# The Mystery of the Egyptian Mummified Kittens

## *Hebony's Odyssey*

*The story of Hebony, a brave little kitten in Old Egypt, and his search for the truth.*

### Dr. Harold Walter Sims Jr.

Fulton Books
Meadville, PA

Published by Fulton Books 2022

ISBN 978-1-63710-028-8 (paperback)
ISBN 978-1-63710-030-1 (hardcover)
ISBN 978-1-63710-029-5 (digital)

Printed in the United States of America

# INTRODUCTION

I am the founder and operator of the American Museum of the House Cat located near Sylva, North Carolina. Soon after I opened the museum in 2017, I acquired an Egyptian cat mummy that had been mummified sometime between 900 and 31 BC. Being an avid cat lover and a history buff, I was haunted by the question, why did the people in Egypt, an advanced civilization, that existed for over three thousand years, worship cats and then sacrifice them to their god Bastet? Searching for an answer sent me on a journey of discovery that lasted over four years and ended with this book. The time is 32 BC. The place is Egypt. Hebony, a four-month-old black kitten, is sent on a mission across the burning sand to find the answer to the same question. And although he never learned an answer, that satisfied my curiosity, his odyssey will take you, the reader, on a literary journey that is a juxtaposition of events of the past and present. Hebony is no ordinary cat, and although he remains a real cat throughout the story, he accomplishes feats that few people could hope to aspire. Alone on his mission, he faces unknown danger as he climbs over mountains of desert sand to learn if a rumor that says little kittens are being raised and mummified to become gifts to their cat goddess Bastet is true. Along the way, he trespasses on property that belongs to the priests. So upset by what he learned, he just can't go home right away. He needs time to think. So he visits the fine city of Alexandria, finds a fisherman who wants him to be the black cat who will bring him good luck, romances a female tabby cat, and attends a chariot race where he meets Grosso, a cat who becomes a friend and his mentor. Hebony goes home with Grosso, and long into the night, they discuss and question the different ways that the cats and people perceive things like competition, risk, becoming a hero, war, and the people's destruction to the environment, since they arrived on the land nine million years after the house cats. Later on, Hebony meets a stranger who lives in an old run-down fisherman's shack deep in the woods. The old man that lives there is a former priest, lonesome for someone to talk to, even if it is a cat. He tells Hebony stories about the history of Egypt, his past, and he reveals that he once worked at the same cat mummy factory that Hebony had found just days before. Upon leaving the old man to his lonesome life, Hebony returns home, reports his finding, and then learns he is being hunted by the priests who were making the cat mummies. He hides in the woods with the wild cats but is forced to enter a town when he becomes plagued with a case of ringworm he contracted by eating uncooked rats. He is captured there and returned to Alexandria where he is tried in a courtroom filled with people wearing the headdresses of many animals, including one dressed as a cat. He is found guilty of the crime treason against the empire by a kangaroo trial in a land where there are no kangaroos, and he is sentenced to death by mummification. But the friends he had made, including the female tabby, Grosso, some local cats, and a nest full of mice, workout a scheme to free him, and he escapes and he runs off into the woods to spend the rest of his life with the female tabby who he had promised that he, unlike other tom cats, will help her raise their kittens. It is a story that will leave you with a new appreciation for cats and a story you will never forget.

# Chapter 1

# A Brief History of the Domestic Cat in Egypt

Reading history educates us as it reveals things that might have happened before we were born. Knowing what happened in the past makes us better able to avoid the mistakes of our forefathers.

As far as the people knew, there had always been small cats in Egypt. Their elders told them that these cats came out of the forest when the people gave up their nomadic lifestyle, settled down, planted crops, built cities, and stored their grain in stone towers or in woven baskets they placed under the floor of their homes.

The skill of fitting stones together close enough to keep out rodents wasn't known at the time, so mice and rats quickly invaded the granaries to obtain easy meals. The cats came to feed on the rodents, but in time, they increased their value by controlling the populations of snakes and scorpions that bit and killed the people. In time, the people found that these cats, unlike any other wildcats they had encountered in the past, were already semidomesticated and friendly.

The children learned this first when they made pets of them, and soon everyone began treating the cats as if they were gods because of the many benefits they provided. Eventually, killing a cat, even by accident, could bring a death sentence to the person foolish or unlucky enough to do so.

Women painted their faces to make themselves look like cats, and they shaved their eyebrows to show their sorrow when a cat died. In the end, even the strongest men treated cats with respect because they protected the crops and made life safer for everyone, and they admitted that these cats were kind of cute and friendly after all.

Later, the people saw even more value in these small cats. As far as people knew at that time, the earth was flat. So when the sun's tiny orange ball disappeared under the edge of the earth at sunset and darkness came, they assumed the sun had gone underground. Being aware that snakes lived under the ground, they feared that a large mythical snake, which they named Apep, might eat the small ball of light and the sun would not rise again to light their day and grow the crops they depended on.

But the elders assured them that Ra, their sun god, took the form of a large cat each night and fought the evil snake by chopping off its many heads. The people believed the elders because every morning, the sun rose again to fill the sky with its light and warmth.

As time went by, the people began to worship cats as deities in both their social and religious practices. In the earliest days of cat worship, the people honored all cats, large and small. The first known cat-headed deity was named Mafdet and was depicted as a leopard. Bastet, a house cat goddess, worshipped as early as 2890 BC, wore a lion's head and remained a deity to almost the end of the empire.

About a hundred years after Bastet's reign began, the remains of a small cat wearing a collar were found in a burial ground at Saqqara. This indicates that the people of Egypt had made pets of some of the small African wildcats. Carvings known as amulets depicting cat heads were made from 2160 to 2000 BC, and later, a cat skeleton and a few small pots that may have stored milk were found in a tomb dating to between 1200 and 1090 BC.

This finding provides even more indication that small cats may have been pets at the time. Throughout later dynasties, cats were depicted on murals, including one with a cat sitting under a chair during a buffet eating either fish or meat. Other depictions show cats hunting game.

Many cat images were carved on the tombs of high-ranking people of importance. One of the first known images was found on the sarcophagus of Prince Thutmose and was said to have been his beloved cat. The goddess Bastet, who had been known since early times, became more popular in about 950 BC and was no longer shown having the head of a lion but that of a small cat (*Felis catus*), a distant relative of our domestic cat.

# CHAPTER 2

# A Rumor Starts

Rumors are stories without all the facts. The only
way to learn their truth is to search for it.

The mummification of all types of animals, including cats, began in
earnest somewhere between 1500 and 664 BC. The cats mummified
at that time were old cats that would be burned at religious ceremo-
nies as we burn candles in our churches today. Others were sold to
people who wanted to use them for personal shrines, and later, pet
cats were mummified for people who wanted their pet to be buried
with them so that its spirit or *ka* could reunite with them in the
afterlife.

But later in history, at a time near the end of the Egyptian
empire, when killing a cat was still a serious crime, there was a rumor
that somewhere in the empire people were killing baby kittens. The
questions were why and where? Many people who heard the rumor
discarded it and said that they hadn't noticed a decrease in the number of cats or kittens. They pointed out that there were cats and kittens everywhere. They shared the homes of people who kept them as
pets, and none of them had mysteriously disappeared. And cats that
were living on the streets were still controlling the snakes and scorpions and protecting the grains from being eaten by rodents.

But the mystery, and the fear that the rumor might be true, a
lie, or maybe just another conspiracy theory, worried the people who

loved cats. They wanted to know where those poor little kittens were coming from and why they were being killed. It didn't seem right that anyone should be allowed to kill kittens when killing any cat, young or old, was still a serious crime. But these people couldn't see any way for anyone to learn the truth.

At the time, travel was almost impossible unless you had a camel to ride or could afford to buy a chariot and a team of horses. The only other way to go anywhere was to walk. But even if these people walked, they had no idea of which way to go, and they were afraid that if they went alone or even in a group, they would be putting themselves in danger of being accused of loitering or trespassing or perhaps be killed by the ones who were killing the kittens, and these people were very well aware that if any of these predictions were to happen to them, it would do nothing to help solve their problem.

Then as they muddled over what they should do next, civil disobedience and protests broke out, and the people divided themselves into two hateful groups: the cat people and the "I hate cats" people. In time, the division between the two factions grew so wide that the two groups no longer spoke to one another, and they crossed the street if they saw a person of the other faction walking along the sidewalk. In an effort to avoid contact, which might have led to violence, the "I hate cats" people started to wear red caps, and the cat people wore green caps so they would be able to identify one another before a meeting led to bloodshed.

# CHAPTER 3

# Shock and Disappointment

Don't let your disappointments stop you. Forget them and go forward.

Despite their division, the two groups had one thing in common: they had faith in their gods and goddesses. Their ruler at the time, between 32 and 31 BC, was Queen Cleopatra, and there was no way for them to have an audience with her. She was much too busy with more important things, like her lover Mark Anthony, to be concerned about the death of a few little kittens. So the next best thing for the people to do was to seek guidance from one of the gods or goddesses they believed in.

Egyptian gods, like all other gods, weren't of flesh and blood, like their rulers the pharaohs. These were gods in the minds of the people. The Egyptians were said to have more gods than any other people ever known. All in all, there were over two thousand different gods or goddesses recognized at the time. The sun god Ra was the most powerful god. He controlled their entire lives. Without sunlight, they could neither grow crops nor find their way during the night. Heka was the god of magic and medicine, and he was thought to have played a part in their creation. Hathor was the goddess of music and dance and so on and so on and so on.

Because Bastet was their cat goddess at the time, it made good sense for them to seek help from her. Bastet stood for all the things they treasured: bountiful harvests, easy childbirth, motherhood, strong, handsome men, and well-minded, healthy children. In the past, they had turned to Bastet whenever there was a need for her guidance. So on the next holy day, the two groups called a truce and came together to pray to Bastet. They told her about the rumor and asked her what she could do about it. They thought she would know the truth, tell them who had started the rumor, put a stop to the killing, ease their minds, and end their division.

But when Bastet answered their prayer, both groups were very surprised when she told them that she was well aware of what was happening. She said she didn't care about it because she enjoyed all the attention she received from the people who brought her little mummified kittens when she made an appearance at the festival along the River Nile in the City of Alexandria or at the annual ritual cat fair held in the city of Bubastis. Then she added, with much excitement and joy in her voice, "Can you believe it? Some of the little cat mummies the people bring me are wrapped in gold leaf and have precious jewels for eyes. I'm a superstar now, and I enjoy when the people sing 'Bastet, Bastet, Superstar' as they cheer and dance around me."

By the time the prayer ended, surprise had turned to disappointment. The people couldn't believe that their favorite goddess, Bastet, had been corrupted by her fame, and they stood together in a state of sheer bewilderment. Some of them, mostly the ones who loved cats, sobbed and cried, wringing their hands and shaking their heads from side to side. When they all regained their composure again, even the ones who had said they hated cats, they got a little misty-eyed over all they had heard. In the end, they all agreed that they needed the cats to control the mice, snakes, and scorpions.

The division between the people was over now, and they were all determined to come together and find a way to learn if the rumor was more than just a rumor and if what Bastet had told them about herself was really true. But then they found that they were between a rock and a hard place; they had to act to solve the mystery or give up and never know the truth.

# CHAPTER 4

# Between a Rock and a Hard Place

> When you're between a rock and a hard place,
> you have to squeeze out from under it and keep
> on going.

It was obvious now that these people weren't going to get any help at all from Bastet, so they went to pray to the only other cat goddess, a little-known goddess named Annipe. Annipe was known to them as the lesser cat goddess who cared for the sick, stray, and abandoned cats.

When Annipe answered their prayer, she said she was sorry to hear about their problem, and although she didn't have much experience in solving problems like theirs, she would do her very best to help them with their investigation. If she found that the rumor was true, she would help them put an end to the killing and then try to figure out what was going on with Bastet.

Then after she took a deep breath, she told them that just the other day she'd been told that there were some strange things going on in a building at the base of a big hill not far from where they lived. She agreed that no person should ever go there and risk life or limb, but if they would wait for a few days, she would try to find a stray cat who would be willing to go inside that building, search around, see what was going on, and return with the information they needed. Annipe said she was well aware that people would be unable to communicate with the cat when it returned but assured them that all gods have the ability to carry on a two-way conversation with cats. As soon as she spoke with the cat, she would pass its findings on to them.

Some of the people were suspicious about the idea that a god could speak with a cat or that a cat could do something that no person could do, but they saw no other choice, and all agreed to go along with her plan.

A few days later, Annipe contacted them again and told them that she had gone around and asked every tomcat she knew to help them, and none were willing to go. She said that some of them even lied to her when they told her that they had female cats to care for or that they were much too busy keeping the streets free of varmints. Annipe knew that was a lie, because tomcats never help a mother cat raise his kittens.

Then she went on to say that all the female cats she knew, turned her down because they were busy raising litters of kittens alone or were much too old to even consider such a thing. But then she said that she remembered a female cat she knew named Nailah that she was certain would help if asked.

Nailah was a cat of great renown who was well-loved for helping others in the past. She had been a street cat when she was younger but now had a safe home on Khufu Street. Even though she was older now, Annipe knew that, sooner or later, Nailah would be giving birth to another litter of kittens. When Annipe asked for her help, Nailah said that she would be more than happy to help them if they could wait until the blessed event occurred.

Then she promised that when one of her newborn kittens reached the age of four months, she would make sure to them that it would be more than qualified and prepared to make the trip and do whatever was necessary to fulfill its assignment.

Of course, this brought up another problem for the people. It had been hard enough for them to believe that an adult cat would be able to do something they couldn't do themselves, but the idea that a little kitten could do it was more than most of them could bear. Some just stood and shook their heads, others argued with one another, and some began to leave the room.

But when they all calmed down enough to learn more about Nailah's promise, Annipe was able to assure them that any one of Nailah's kittens would be more than qualified to go on such a mission because her kittens were always so much larger than usual, very attractive, more intelligent, and much braver than any other kittens ever known.

So, in the end, they all agreed to let Nailah choose the kitten that she thought would be the one most able to go on their mission, learn who was doing the killing, why they were killing innocent little kittens, and if it had the time, try to find out if Bastet had really become a superstar because of it. Then, with a few minor reservations from some people who suggested that a dog might be able to do a better job, they put their differences aside and placed their problem into the mind of Annipe and the paws of the brave little kitten Nailah would send to go in search of the truth and return with enough information to put a stop to whatever was going on.

# CHAPTER 5

# The Birth of Hebony

Every life begins with birth. After that, what we
do in life is up to us.

When Nailah's four kittens were born a few weeks later, the firstborn
was a male, and he was the largest and most active of the kittens she
had given birth to. She named him Hebony, their word for black,
because the wisps of fur on his tiny naked body were jet-black.

A black coat of fur on a cat was quite out of the ordinary, and
the few cats that were born with black coats usually didn't survive
into adulthood. That was because their color made them easily seen
by larger animals, like jackals, who hunted them and ate the ones
they caught. But the dark color pleased Nailah because she knew that
a black cat, if it were careful, would be much better able to enter the
cat mummy making complex under the cover of darkness and learn
what was going on. Nailah was sure Hebony's color had come from
divine intervention.

Hebony's eyes and ears were not open at birth, and Nailah knew
she would have to wait about three or four weeks before she could
communicate with him. So she went about life as usual, nursing her
kittens, keeping them warm and clean, and telling them that she
loved them. But Nailah could hardly wait until all her kittens were
able to walk and play. When Hebony's eyes opened a little after fourteen days, Nailah saw that his eyes were blue, the color of all newborn

kittens' eyes. Now she knew that within a little over a week, he would be able to hear and understand what she wanted to say to him.

But when that time came, all the kittens were still nursing, and they rarely ventured away from the nest. If she spoke to Hebony when the other kittens were around, they would hear what she was saying to him, and she didn't want any of them to think they were any less important than he was. So despite her eagerness to tell Hebony then, she decided to wait until all her kittens were older, not nursing as much, and for a time when she and Hebony could be alone together.

# CHAPTER 6

# What Would His Mission Be?

Every mission in life should be to do something
that will make the world a better place.

When Hebony reached the age of four weeks, his eyes had opened wide. Now they were the color gold, like those of the leopard, and their pupils were as black as obsidian and sparkled like diamonds in a beam of sunlight. Nailah knew golden eyes were the best for night vision, and she was glad that Hebony had been blessed with them. She was sure they would help him find his way in the darkness.

Several weeks later, when Hebony was a little older and all the other kittens had gone away to play "chase my tail," Nailah went to him. She told him that before he was born, the goddess Annipe had asked her to choose one of her kittens to go on a dangerous mission, and although she loved all of her kittens very much, she had chosen him. She said that if he were successful on the mission, he could save the lives of many little kittens.

She told him that she was certain she had made the right choice because he had shown that he was curious, adventurous, caring, energetic, and had a memory that was more than amazing. But even though he had been born with gifts that very few kittens are blessed with, he would still have to work hard and be prepared in both mind and body to be able to complete this mission.

But it seemed Hebony hadn't been paying much attention to what she had been saying, because toward the end of their conversation, he rolled over onto his back, opened his eyes wide, and looked up at her in bewilderment. When a small scarab beetle ran in front of him, he jumped up and chased the bug around the room. He told her he wanted to play now and not talk anymore. The conversation was over, and Nailah knew she would have to wait and tell him again when he was older.

But a few days later, he surprised her when he came to her and said that despite the dangers he might have to face, he would like to know more about the mysterious mission she said he would be going on. Apparently, he had listened to more of their conversation than she had thought. This made her more certain that she had made the right choice and that Hebony truly no ordinary cat. But then just to be sure he was fully understood what she had said to him a few days ago, she repeated everything once again and then went on to tell him what would be expected of him when he went on the mission. This time, Hebony sat very still, and he listened to every word she said, and when she was through, he told her that he was very excited about going on the mission, and he said that he would do his very best to carry out the assignment and return with enough information to solve the mystery and stop killing the baby kittens. Then he stood up, and as he started to walk away, he turned back and told her that he was going to do it under the cover of darkness so nobody could see him. Nailah laughed about what he said and called him back and told him, "I think you'd like to make a better life for those other little kittens. The gods have offered you a purpose for living, and I'm glad that you are willing to accept it. Most of us have to find our purpose in life later in life. I hope that when your brothers and sisters grow up, they will find something that they want to do and then go on to pursue it." Hebony nodded, said thank you, and then he lay down and took a nap.

# CHAPTER 7

# Why We All Need Purpose in Our Lives

A purpose is a map you draw in your mind and follow to where you want to go.

Nailah was very pleased that Hebony felt the way he did about being given a purpose in life, but she also was aware that although most kittens find a purpose sooner or later, but some spend their lives playing and never do much else. She knew that without having a purpose in life, no one could ever be truly happy because they have nothing to look forward to. Having a purpose makes your life worth living. She knew that little kittens weren't expected to find a purpose in their lives until they are much older than Hebony, but the gods had asked her to offer him a purpose, and she was glad that he accepted it. Discussing the purpose of his life had been hard for Hebony to understand, but Nailah was aware of that and she would take every opportunity to encourage him to live up to his purpose as he grew older.

Hebony slept well throughout the night because he was happy about what his mother told him, and he was glad that she had asked him if he would accept what the gods had offered. He had many pleasant dreams that night, and he slept until late the next morning without waking up.

# CHAPTER 8

# Growing Up

Growing up is the time between birth and becoming an adult. Use that time preparing to do something great.

Hebony spent the next four weeks growing up, playing with his littermates, learning to walk without falling over, and sleeping a lot. Up until then, his mother had cared for all of them in every way that she could. But when her milk began to dry up and she knew she would not be able to nurse them much longer, she started bringing them mice she had killed. It was time for them to learn to eat solid food. At first, they didn't know what to do with a dead mouse. They played with it like a toy, tossing it up in the air and batting it around the nest with their front paws.

When they got tired, they went back to nursing for the milk that was left, and she ate the mouse herself. A few days later, she got up while her kittens were still nursing, left them in the nest, and walked a short distance away from them and called for them to follow her, and led them to a dead mouse she had left hidden in a patch of grass and gathered them around it. Then they watched as she showed them how to butcher it. It was a messy job, and they all said that they thought that nursing was a much better way to eat, but in time, they were asking her to show them another mouse. Soon they were following her wherever she went hunting, and in a very short time, they learned to kill mice she had injured. Then it wasn't long before they learned to catch, kill, and butcher healthy mice for themselves.

# CHAPTER 9

# Separation and the Fear of Loneliness

There comes a time in life when we all must leave childhood and become an adult.

The time had come when Nailah knew she would soon have to stop taking care of this litter of kittens. It's something all mother cats must do when they learn that they will soon have a new litter to care for. She knew she couldn't take care of new little baby kittens and care for the older ones that would soon be ready to leave the nest and go off on their own. So one night, as these kittens were nursing, even though her milk had almost dried up, she stood up and walked away from them. She turned back reluctantly and watched them playing in their little nest.

It was time to tell them they must leave her soon, and she hated to have to do it. She'd told this to other kittens in the past, and each time, it became harder for her to do. She thought she might be able to wait and tell these kittens a little later, but the movement of unborn kittens inside her belly told her the time had come for them to stop nursing and learn to take care of themselves. Female cats have many litters of kittens each year, and the number can be many more than ten. But unlike other animals, nursing doesn't stop cats from having new kittens growing inside them while they nurse the kittens they already have. Nailah was not a young cat. She had had many kittens during her long life, and she knew she would have many more before her time was up. It was always hard for her to say goodbye to her kittens and send them out into the world alone.

She came to love each of her babies, and she knew that when they left her, it was unlikely she would ever see them again and she wondered if they would recognize her if they did. At times, she wished she was too old to have any more kittens. It didn't seem fair that female cats had to spend the best years of their lives raising kittens while a male cat chose what he wanted to do with his life. In a way, she was envious of her son, Hebony. He would be going on a mission, and despite the danger he might face, she wished she was going instead. Telling Hebony and his siblings' they would have to leave her soon was going to be extra hard this time.

But it had to be done, so she went to her kittens and told them to stop playing and come close to her. Then maybe because she was so upset about having to tell them she must leave them so soon, or maybe it was because she was just sick and tired of taking care of them for such a long time, she said to them in a somewhat nasty way, "I want you all to know that soon I will be leaving you, and you will be all alone. It's time for you to learn how to take care of yourselves." Then, without a word of comfort she walked away. Later that day, she felt bad about the way she'd spoken to them, but it was something her instincts told her she must do. Nature dictates that all kittens must grow up and someday get along without having a mother.

All the kittens were upset by what she had said, but hearing the words about her not being with them any longer was especially hard for Hebony to understand. He knew he would soon be going on a very dangerous mission, and he began to worry that his mother might leave him before he had to go. He wanted her to be there to help him get ready. He needed her to encourage him, and he was even more worried that she might not be there when he returned. He knew he had to do what he'd been born to do, but he didn't understand what loneliness was. Until then, he had never experienced being lonely.

He knew he wasn't going to mind being separated from his littermates if that was all it meant. They'd started to annoy him anyway. He had thought many times that his life would be better without them. Then he would have his mother all to himself. He'd already tried several times to lead them away from the nest to a dark corner of the room, where they'd get lost, but they always found their way back. If they didn't, they would listen for the calls of their mother and follow them back to her.

Being alone in the world was hard enough for any young kitten, but when he thought of going on a long mission all alone, his heart beat faster. Hebony tried hard to suppress the thought and wished that his mother had brought up the subjects of loneliness and separation sooner, at a time when she could have explained what it meant. Now he was fearful about going on his mission and he wasn't sure he wanted to make that treacherous trip after all. He didn't sleep well that night. He tossed and turned, haunted by the ghosts and jackals that chased him through the dark hours of his dreams.

# Chapter 10

# Encouragement for Hebony

We all like a little encouragement for the things
we want to do.

The next morning, when the other kittens had gone out to play,
Hebony waited for his mother to return from hunting mice. He
wanted to talk to her about separation and loneliness. He had no
doubt that he was her favorite son and that their relationship knew
no depths, and he felt sure that she would understand his concerns
and fear. So when his mother came into the room carrying a dead
mouse, he went to her and asked her to put the mouse down and
explain to him what she meant when she said she would be leaving
them all alone. Nailah put down the mouse and took a little time to
groom herself.

When she gained her composure, she asked him to sit next to
her. She explained that all kittens must leave home when they reach
a certain age and that each of them must go their own way. That
could be going on a dangerous mission like he would be doing. Or it
could be becoming a grown-up cat that would help control rodents,
be someone's pet, or becoming a tomcat that would, well, let's say,
just being a tomcat.

"It doesn't matter what you do with your life. It's how well you
do it," she said.

She told him again that she knew he would do what was right and that he would be successful. He would find where and why the kittens were being killed and disclose the information, then the people would try to have it closed down. By doing so, he would save the lives of many little kittens. Then she said, "Don't worry, I'll be here when you come back. This is your home."

Nailah's kind words made Hebony feel better, and his fears faded as he let them slip out of his mind. Then he stood up and walked to the other side of the room and sat with his back to her, licking his paw and thinking. He turned his head toward hers and told her he was glad that she said she would be there when he returned. He told her he would keep his purpose in mind and think positively about the trip.

# CHAPTER 11

# What His Inner Thoughts Would Mean

It doesn't matter what you think about; the outcome depends on what you achieve.

After hearing Hebony's remark about keeping positive, his mother
called him to her side again and told him she wanted to explain how
his attitude and his thoughts could affect the success of his mission.

"Hebony," she said, "positive or negative thoughts don't really
matter. You have to be realistic about the things you can and can't
do. You'll have to think positive thoughts if you really want to go
through with your mission, but you will have to deal with your negative thoughts as well. Having negative thoughts shows that you are
aware that things could go wrong. Then, if and when they do, you
will be ready to use what I call a 'What if factor' and be ready to deal
with them. Staying positive is good, but you have to be ready to deal
with the little what ifs when they come up. You have to have a plan
in mind to overcome any obstacle that may come your way. But you
should always err on the side of caution and not take any unneces-
sary chances. Be realistic about everything. Things are bound to go
wrong. You must make yourself ready in body and mind to go for the
goal and work hard to complete your mission come what may.

"Success comes from planning, hard work, and then most of all, action. The end result will depend on how well you planned, how well-prepared you were, and how strong your commitment was. Keep your mind on the goal and don't allow other thoughts to get in your way. When your mission is over, you will have time to do other things. Do your best and hope that Lady Luck and destiny will be on your side. Your success could make life better for other kittens."

When she turned and walked away, Hebony wasn't sure he understood everything his mother had told him. So when he went to bed that night, he began thinking about the trip and about all the things that might go wrong.

*What if I came to a hill I thought was too hard for me to climb over?* he thought to himself. *Would I give up? No, I would search for other hills that lie in the same direction and find one that I could climb. What if I didn't find another one? I'd go back and find a way to get over the first hill I found. I would never give up.*

He rolled over, thought of a few more bad things that could go wrong, and told himself that he would find a way to overcome all of them. Then he relaxed, and as he tried to go to sleep, he thought about all the good things that might happen He finally came to the conclusion that for him to have success and finish what he'd started, he would have to just do his very best, have self-confidence, keep the goal in mind, be persistent, and above all, not give up even if others told him it couldn't be done. Then he remembered his mother telling him about good luck, He'd heard somewhere that black cats were lucky, so with that in mind, he closed his eyes, rolled over, and went to sleep, hoping that old Lady Luck would be on his side.

# Chapter 12

# Learning the Ways of a Cat

A pep talk and a learning experience.

It had been only a few weeks since Nailah had brought up the subject of her to leave when her new kittens were born. It had been a shock to them, but now that that was over and done, it was time for these kittens to be told what they needed to know and be aware of when they were grown-up. This would include being able to keep themselves clean.

Her kittens were three months old, and they would soon have to leave the nest. She lined them up across the room from her and told them to watch her and listen to what she said. She knew that kittens, even those that might have lost their mother, learned the habits of a cat on their own, but Hebony would be going off on his mission alone, and she wanted to be sure he knew how to take care of himself before he left. But before she did that, she said she wanted to tell them a story she told to all her other kittens when they were about their age.

She started by saying, "Cats have many special abilities. They have the ability to speak with and understand the language of any other animal they meet, except that of the people. If you ever meet one, you'll find that you will be able to understand what a person says to you, but sadly, they will not be able to understand a word you say to them. Your mew or a meow means nothing to them. In most cases, when you meow, they assume you're hungry, and they will offer you some of their food to eat. When they do, be kind to them. They can't help being so unfortunate. Try to eat a little of what they've offered to you, and then if you don't like it, you don't have to eat it all. But it is good to eat just a little. That makes them think you're not hungry because you've been eating a lot of mice lately. That's the only thing a lot of them think cats are good for.

"Cats lived in the wild long before the people came to this land. When the people first came, they wandered from place to place and lived in caves. We didn't have much to do with them back then. We each lived our separate lives.

As a rule, cats didn't live with the people when they lived in caves, and I don't think the adults made them into made pets. Maybe a child would find a little lost kitten and make a pet of it, but when the family moved to a new cave, most kittens were lost along the way, and in time, the child forgot about it. But you don't need to worry most of these kittens would have been old enough to use the skills they'd acquired and survive wherever they were dropped. And there were lots of cats around back then, and one of the mother cats in the area would have heard the kitten crying and would have cared for it. A mother cat, with milk, will rescue any lost kittens and raise them as one of their own. A male lion will eat any kittens, that aren't his own, but male house cats don't do that. Male cats don't bring food to a mother cat, or help her raise the kittens, but they don't eat her kittens. Cat mothers are super mothers. And there were lots of cats around, and if a mother cat heard it crying, she would care for it. Most any mother cat would rescue a lost kitten and care for it. A male cat could never raise a kitten, but one might protect a lost kitten until a female cat came along.

Later, when the people gave up their nomadic life and settled in cities, the cats decided to join them when they found that the people were growing seasonal grains and were storing the dry grain under their home or in towers built of loosely fitted stones. The mice had already come into town to eat the grain that spilled out, and the cats came to eat the mice. Cats have always been curious little animals, and when they find something that's better than what they had, they take advantage of it. Living in the city where the mice were fat, and easier to catch, was much better than it was out in the wild where the cats had to chase skinny mice and catch them before they could eat them. That was hard work.

Long before the cats had come into town, the people had had already taken the wild camels and horses, out of the wild, and trained them to pull their carts and carry things on their backs. These wild animals didn't like it, but they submitted to it. But when the people tried to train the cats to work for them, they soon learned that, beyond a few tricks, the cats would do to please them, they weren't going to train them to do much else. And whenever they tried, the cat just got up and walked away. Remember, you're special you're a cat and you can walk alone. You don't need people. But the people need you; they can't even catch their own mice.

When Nailah said the people couldn't even catch their own mice, the kittens all laughed and began to fidget around, so she stopped talking and gave them a chance to stretch their legs or do other business they needed to do. Then she continued.

"Cats never traveled in herds or packs because cats don't need another cat to help them hunt and catch their food. Cats hunt alone, and they are known as an ambush predator. They hide in the brush, and when they see something they can eat, like a fat mouse, they sneak from bush to bush, and when they get close enough, they pounce on the mouse and hold it with their teeth until it dies.

"And then, if they weren't really hungry before they killed the mouse, they would toss it up in the air just for the fun of it. It's a playtime thing, and it scares the devil out of any other mice that might be watching. Even old cats do this. Cats are happy animals. Maybe it's because they never allowed the people to make slaves of them.

"When playtime is over, they take their time eating but never share their food with other cats unless it's one of their kittens. As I said, cats are loners. They walk and hunt alone. If you remember what I teach you, you will be able to live alone in the wild if you need to. You must never forget your skills. And one more thing I want you to know about the people is that I don't think they are very satisfied

31

with their lot in life. They want the things other people have, and they fight wars and kill one another to get what they want. They change the land to please themselves, change the flow of rivers to grow their crops, and dump piles of trash everywhere.

"And they don't even bury their waste like we do. And the people don't seem to fit into any category like the other animals do. People do form herd-like groups among their friends and family but then they pick a leader with a big mouth who tells them what to do and when to do it. They don't have much self-esteem or really want to think for themselves.

"They blindly follow their leader, distrust the people in all the other small herds around them, isolate themselves from one another, and end up fighting wars against each other. I'm afraid that, in time, the people will destroy the land as we know it. Their history is written on the battlefields. Someday they might destroy the land. So you'll need to keep your skills up to date so you will be able to survive on what they've left behind. Then the cats could live off the land again and live in harmony with the land like the cats did before the people came. In all my life, I have never heard any stories about cats raising armies and waging war against one another. All the animals, especially the people, need to love one another and live in peace and harmony."

Nailah stopped talking then and sent the four kittens to sit on the other side of the room. "Now listen to what I say and watch what I do. You'll need to know how to wash and groom your fur when you grow up. We learn things by observation. I want you to watch how I wash and groom myself. You may want to make changes to suit yourself later, but we have to start somewhere. So we'll begin by washing our paws."

Nailah washed one of her front paws and said, "Now you'll have to wet your tongue to wash and groom all the rest of the parts of your body, but your paws must be clean before you start. Now this might not sound appetizing to you, but you must use your tongue to clean your paws before you start. Your tongue has little bumps on it that will help with cleaning and grooming. Be sure to clean each paw way down deep, and in between your toes, spread your toes wide to be sure you get that bumpy tongue way down deep in between your toes, to the very bottom."

All the kittens looked at her with disgust as they watched her lick her paw to demonstrate. Then with reservation, they each tried to follow her instructions. It was easy for them to clean their front paws. All they had to do was to sit on their bottom, lift one paw, and lick it. The back paws were harder because until they learned how to balance themselves when they lifted a hind paw, they fell over. When they tried it, some of them fell over several times, but after a few attempts, they got the knack of it and were soon having fun licking a hind paw and then falling over just for the fun of it.

Nailah smiled at their antics and told them they needed to pay more attention to what they were doing. Then she told them that they would hardly ever need to wash with the back paws because they were mainly used to scratch where it itches. That made them smile. Next, she taught them how to wash their face.

"Now sit on your bottom and put your tail out behind you for balance, spread your hind legs apart a little, and bring a front paw up to your mouth and lick it to get it wet. Then reach it up to your face and wash it around and around. It will take several strokes before you're done. When you're satisfied with one side, wet your other paw and do the same on the other side. Good. Now wet both paws and twist your wrist so you are able to wash the very top of your head. You might not be able to bend your arm enough to wash up there because it takes a little wrist action to get the paw in the right places, so wet your paw and wrist, lean your head toward that side, and wash around on top of your head and behind your ears. And remember, you won't be able to do a good job without some wrist action."

They quickly learned to do one side, and without being told, they did the same on the other side. "Oh, you're such smart kittens," she said to encourage them.

But when she stopped talking, she noticed that Hebony was still washing the top of his head. She looked at him, turned her head side to side to indicate no-no, and added, "You too, Hebony."

Hebony, who was the clown of her litter, smiled back at her and quickly brought his paw down to the floor. Then he sat up straight like the rest of them.

"Now it is time to do something easy," she said. "Now I want you to lay on your back with your tail out behind you. Wet your front paws one at a time, and then by using your tongue and a wet paw, you will be able to wash all over your tummy. You just have to bend your neck down and then swing your head from side to side as you wash over your chest to your tail. Along the way, you might want to reach, and don't forget to wash and groom the insides of your legs. Then, if you lift your upper body and sit up a little, you will be able to reach over and groom your tail."

Learning these positions took a little time for them to get things right, and sometimes one of them leaned too far and fell over, but they were always able to get upright again and go on washing and grooming. When they were finished, they all said that washing their tummy made them laugh because it tickled. Now it was time for lunch, and even though they had been weaned a long time ago, she let them nurse because they had been so good.

Soon, they all laid down to rest, and Nailah told them that learning how to groom the rest of their bodies would be covered at another time.

# Chapter 13

# Nailah Explains What Adult
# Life May Be Like

We all need a little help becoming a grown-up.

Several days later, Nailah gathered her four kittens around her again. It was time to teach them more about grooming themselves, but she'd noticed they were doing so well with that, so she instead decided to ask them what they wanted to do when they grew up.

Hebony piped up right away and said, "I'm going on a mission."

"Yes, Hebony," she replied. "You were given the mission by the gods, but you might want to think about what you'd like to do after that. The mission shouldn't take all your life. At least we hope it won't. So I'd like to know if you have thought about another goal for the rest of your life."

Hebony sat up and started to groom himself and then asked, "What do other cats do when they grow up?"

Then all the other kittens spoke up all at once saying, "We don't know that either. We don't know what cats are expected to do or what they can do when they are grown up."

It was a good question, and Nailah had to take a little time to think before she gave them an answer.

"It depends on a lot of things," she said. "There are always people who want little kittens or even older cats to come into their homes and become their pets. Being a pet is not such a bad life. They feed you and keep you safe from harm, but it may have some drawbacks. Some people have little children at home who might not know how to be nice to a cat and they might pull your tail. If they do, cry, and they will let go.

"But if they are nice and have been taught how to play with a cat, you just have to be nice back to them. If you enjoy what the children are doing, roll over on your back and wiggle your tummy. Children like to rub a cat's tummy, and if you purr, that will make them very, very happy. When you get tired of playing, you just have to stand up and walk away and take a nap. When you do that, most children will think of something else they can do, like go outside and play."

Hebony asked, "Can I go outside and play too? That sounds like fun."

Then his mother replied, "Maybe, but if you leave their yard and get lost, you might wish you hadn't."

Then she went on with the lesson because she didn't know what Hebony might ask next. He had a habit of asking too many questions. She admired him for that, but she wanted to get on with the lesson now.

"There is another thing you need to know about if you're going to be a pet. Most women like cats. We think it's because of their maternal instinct. They see cats as little babies and treat them as such. If you're sweet to them, they will spoil you and give you all kinds of love. Some men, on the other hand, don't see cats the same way women do. These men want to be in charge of everything, and they will try their best to dominate you. You have to understand this and try to change their attitude. You have to train them to make them love you. You do this by ignoring them at first. These men don't like to be ignored, and sometimes they will offer you treats when the women aren't watching. That will be your chance to win them over. Be nice to them, and sooner or later, they will become fond of you. Most men really like cats, but some don't want their friends to think that they aren't the boss of everything in their house."

Then she went on to say, "But not all cats become pets. Some will become street cats and find a life that suits them. Having a good life on the street depends a lot on whether you're a male or female. Female cats will have little choice. They spend most of their time raising kittens and will have little time for much else until they are too old to have any more. Male cats have a role in making kittens too, but they rarely, if ever, do anything to help raise them."

"They usually follow the role of their fathers and leave the mother long before the kittens are born," she said with disgust in her voice. "Male cats leave raising kittens to the mother. Then for the rest of their lives, these tomcats roam the streets, keeping them free of rodents and bragging about all the female cats they've ever known. And they all do that until the day they die."

Nailah had little respect for tomcats. Hebony looked away and laughed as she frowned at him, and then she went on with her lecture.

"About all old female cats can do, once they can no longer have kittens, is to find a nice home or temple where there is food and shelter and maybe a place where they can help younger cats raise their kittens. Older cats, even some male cats, make good babysitters."

Hebony laughed and looked up at his mother. Then he told her he was sorry he had laughed so much and replied, "When I grow up, I'm going to change things like that and help my mother cat raise my kittens."

Nailah overlooked the "my" part of what he said and told him it might be nice if he did that, but in order to do it, he would have to change an age-long tradition that all male cats live by.

Hebony turned to her again, smiled, and said, "Did you know that male and female storks stay together all of their lives and raise their babies together?"

Nailah turned her head away. She didn't have an answer for that one, so she just walked away mumbling to herself and saying, "Hebony, you are, for sure, no ordinary cat."

One day, although her other three kittens hadn't asked, Nailah thought it was time to tell them why she had chosen Hebony to go on the mission. She didn't want them to think that the decision was hers alone. She took them aside and explained it was because the gods wanted her to choose the largest kitten in her litter and the one best suited to survive such a rigorous assignment. Hebony, she told them, was, by far, the largest kitten she ever had, and because of that, he would be better able to climb up hills and over the sandy dunes and dig deep into the sand if a sandstorm were coming. His larger body would cope better during the heat of the day and cold nights, and Hebony's size alone would scare off most all the wild animals, like big cats, wild dogs, jackals, and puff adders, who hunted for their prey, and cats were high on their menu. She said it was a hard choice for her to make and that she was sad that she had to do it, but in the end, the gods had approved of what she did. When she finished her explanation, they felt better about it because now they knew they wouldn't have to face any such dangers, but later that day, some of them still wished they could go because Hebony was going to go where no cat had ever gone before. But by the end of the day, they all seemed to agree that Hebony should be the one, and they said it was okay by them if he went alone.

# CHAPTER 14

# Hebony Gets Help from His Family

It's never fun to learn alone.

Later that day, his siblings told Hebony they understood why their mother had chosen him for the dangerous mission and that they would like to help him get ready to go. The two boys Aten and Kamuzu and the girl named Khari worked hard to help Hebony get into shape. The very next day, they walked around the yard and placed some stones near each tree or other landmark they could find as Hebony watched from where he stood in the shade of a magnolia tree. When the three were satisfied with the exercise track they had carefully laid out, they called for Hebony to come and see what they had done.

Hebony got up from his shady place under the tree and walked over to them.

"Why are you putting rocks around the yard?" Hebony asked.

"It's a track for you to run around so you can be in shape to go on your mission," Aten said. "I think you should run around several times each day. We'll run with you, just in case one of us has to go in your place."

Hebony slowly glanced around the yard, staring at each little pile of rocks.

"I don't see the need for me to run around in a circle. Mom said I was the best qualified to go on the mission," Hebony said. "She didn't say I needed to get into shape to do it. You don't need to get in shape either. I'm the only one that's going. Mom said that too."

Later that day, Hebony went to talk with his mother and told her what Aten said.

"I'm sorry Aten feels that way," his mother said, "but I agree that you need to get into shape before you go. You need to get rid of some of that baby fat you have around your tummy. No cat could go on a trip like yours unless they were in tip-top shape. You're going to have to climb hills of sand, and maybe you'll need to outrun a jackal."

The part about the jackal impressed Hebony. That was the one thing that everyone had warned him about.

"Don't let Aten bother you, Hebony," his mother said. "He's just a little jealous. He'll get over it. Go back and tell them you'll at least try to get into shape. I think you will thank them all when you're in the middle of a steep hill and getting tired."

So each morning, Hebony ran beside his siblings to gain the stamina they told him he needed. They helped him become faster than a monkey climbing up trees, and each evening, they played hide and seek together so he could learn to hide from danger and would be very hard to find if he was hiding from someone.

# CHAPTER 15

# Nailah Returns from a
# Night on the Town

All mothers need some time alone.

One morning, when Hebony was high up in a tree chasing invisible monkeys, his mother came back from a trip into town. His three siblings saw her coming and shouted to Hebony, who was up in the tree at the time.

"Remember, Hebony, the first rule of tree climbing is that cats always climb up and down trees heads up."

Then they ran to greet their mother.

Nailah told them that she just learned that she was going to have another litter of kittens and that she wouldn't be able to stay with them much longer. It was a shock to them, but by now, the kittens were older. They had been told what cats were supposed to do, and they were ready to be on their own. So they brushed off what she had told them and went back to help Hebony get down from the tree.

The incident was soon forgotten, and his three siblings cheered when he made it down from the tall tree with only one small mistake. They didn't tell Hebony what his mother had just told them. They thought it might worry him, and they were sure their mother would do her best to stay long enough to see him off on the trip.

# CHAPTER 16

# Hebony Explores the Desert

It is always wise to know where you're going.

The time for Hebony to leave on his mission was near. But up until then, he had not ventured far from home. His siblings had been helping him get in shape, and although they ran together every day, they had not gone beyond the edge of the grassy lawn that surrounded their home.

One day, his brother Aten said, "I think we should go out and explore the desert. Maybe we could find one of those big hills you told us about, like the one you might have to climb over someday. When you see one, you might want to change your mind."

Hebony had forgotten if he'd ever told Aten about the hills, but he agreed it was a good idea. But he had been a little upset with Aten lately, and although Aten had helped him get into shape, Hebony thought Aten had been acting sort of cold toward him lately. Hebony wanted to be friends with Aten. He was one of his two brothers, so he thought he should talk about this with him when they went together to explore the lands beyond.

At first, the two brothers couldn't see much of interest beyond their grassy lawn. But as they entered the desert, they found that the vast unknown was much larger than they'd expected. Rolling hills of sand seemed to go on and on forever, and there was very little sign of any vegetation. There were no trees, and what plants there grew too low to the ground. Hebony tagged along behind Aten, acting like he wasn't impressed.

When he stopped to nibble on some small blades of grass, Aten walked on, and Hebony had to run to catch up with him.

"I wouldn't have to know how to climb trees if the deserts are all like this." Hebony said to Aten. "I could run through this grass and jump over the few little bushes we've seen. I don't think I could hide anywhere either." So much for playing hide and seek all those times. And I'd better leave very early in the morning when I start on my mission. I couldn't walk very far if the sand was this hot. My feet are burning up."

"Oh, come on, Hebony. Stop fussing so much," Aten answered. "And quit being negative. It's not that hot. I could walk on the sand like this all day. Maybe I should go on your mission."

Hebony didn't answer, and the two walked on in silence. But as they went farther away from home, the animosity between them seemed to lessen, and they joked together about a tiny mouse that scurried out of one bush to another and agreed it wouldn't have made much of a meal.

Then Hebony ran ahead of his brother and took the lead.

"Look over there!" Hebony shouted. "There's a tree-covered hill over there. And without waiting for Aten to answer, he shouted, "Follow me! It doesn't look very far away."

Aten didn't answer, but he followed Hebony in the direction of the hill. But as they came nearer, they saw that the hill was beyond a group of large sand dunes that rose far up from a flat desert floor. Hebony looked at the dunes and suggested they change their direction.

"You can't do that when you're on your mission. You can't let a few little hills of sand get in your way," Aten said.

Hebony turned and looked at him, pointed his hand to the left, and replied, "Oh look, there's a group of odd-looking trees over there. Let's go that way. It looks like all the branches on those trees hang down from the top. And look, I think I see a water hole near them. I could sure use a drink. How about you?"

Aten decided to stop badgering Hebony and followed him toward the water hole. As they came closer, they noticed that there were large animals standing in the shade of the trees. The animals were light brown in color, and there were very large bumps on their backs. When the brothers came closer, the strange animals made loud noises and stamped their feet. They were the largest animals they'd ever seen, and they were so frightened that they left the water hole without taking a drink.

When they arrived home, the two brothers each went their own way. Aten disappeared into the house, and Hebony went to find his mother and tell her about the things they'd seen and discussed the fear he felt when he came to the group of sand dunes at the base of the mountain. He also wanted to tell her about Aten's animosity toward him. But when he found her, she was busy with other things, and she told him he would have to wait until she was finished.

Hebony spent the time cleaning his fur and getting the sand from between his toes. This gave him time to think about what he would say to her, and as he did, he came to the conclusion that some of it could wait until after he made the trip. He'd committed to going on the mission by himself, and if he brought his concerns about Aten's feelings up, she might think that he was having second thoughts about going. It really didn't matter to him what Aten thought. He was the one who was going to solve the mystery.

So when she came to him, he just told her that they had learned a lot about the desert, and he asked her about the big animals they had seen by the water hole, he'd already decided not to bring up anything more about Aten.

She explained that they were camels and that they wouldn't harm anyone on purpose then warned him not to get too close to one of them because they could kick and spit stinky black stuff in his face. Hebony added that bit of knowledge to his mental list of the things he wanted to remember if he ever saw a camel again.

# CHAPTER 17

# Which Way to Go

Everything in life needs a plan and a direction.

But as he started to leave the room, he stopped and asked his mother which way he should go when he began his journey. Nailah was at a loss for words. She hadn't thought about that until then. She didn't know the answer. So she told him she would think about it, and she went to a quiet place to think. When she couldn't come up with the answer herself, she called on the God Annipe and asked her what to do. Annipe was very upset and said it was something they all should have thought about long before now.

She apologized to Nailah and agreed that there was no way any cat, even a smart cat like Hebony, could go on a mission if he didn't know which way to go. Lucky for him, the Egyptians had many other animal gods. The falcon god was one of the earliest. His name was Horus, and his domain was the sky. He could fly above the landscape; he was the avenger of wrongs and the defender of law and order. No one could have been any better than Horus to search for a possible location. So they asked Horus to fly above the lands near Hebony's home and search for a building that might be the place where kittens were being killed. Horus was more than willing to help. He flew around most of the time anyway, and he loved being carried up high into the sky on the sun-warmed thermals that rose up from the hot desert sand below.

Horus told her he could not believe that the cat god Basset had let them all down and then said he was very familiar with most of the local landscape. After making several sorties over the desert, he returned with his findings and told Annipe that he had seen something that he had noticed a long time ago, and just out of curiosity, he'd been following its changes ever since. It was a group of large buildings made of wood, and the complex had grown larger each time he'd seen it. He said it was just off the road to Alexandria and was only just a short distance from the place Hebony lived.

Horus suggested that Hebony should start his journey by climbing up a rough trail that leads to the top of the large tree-covered hill right behind their home. He said it would be a long climb to the top, but when he reached it, he would be able to see the buildings down below. Then he added that because fog shrouded the top of the hill, most of the time, he' had never had a good look at its top or seen if there was a good trail down the other side. He told Annipe to wish Hebony luck and to tell him to be careful.

Annipe told Horus she was grateful for his service and the information he'd provided, and then she thanked him for his help. A few days later, Nailah told Hebony that she had learned of a possible location of what might be the mummy processing plant and that it was just over the hill behind their house.

Now Hebony would be able to begin his mission with the knowledge of its possible location. Hebony was happy knowing he had a plan to follow. He was ready to get going now, and he looked forward to the day he would leave.

# Chapter 18

# Hebony's Trip Begins

Every journey begins with a single step.

By now, Hebony was a little over five months old and weighed about five and a half pounds. He had worked his body into shape for the trip. He felt he was ready to go, and he was committed. He couldn't turn back without being a coward, and cats are never cowards. The night before he was to leave, his mother said to him and said, "Be brave and courageous, believe in yourself, have self-confidence, and never think of turning back. Your mission is to make the future better for all kittens, not only the ones you might save there, but for all the kittens throughout the empire. You must find where they get the kittens from, the ones they use to make mummies, and return with the truth."

After her encouragement, they had a family party, and everybody wished Hebony well and hoped he would have a safe trip. Then, everyone went to the place in their home to sleep. But Hebony didn't go to bed right away. He sat beside his bed and worried that he might not be able to do what he had been chosen for. He thought about waking his mother to have the last talk about his doubts and fear but discarded the idea. He didn't want to worry her any more than she already was. He remembered her saying that everyone had done all they could to help him. Now it was up to him.

When he finally crawled into the little reed basket, he tossed and turned for a long time. When sleep did come, it didn't last very long. Nightmares about the dangers he might face and the fear that one of them might end his life plagued him through the night. But each time, he made himself go back to sleep by telling himself that he could and he would do what must be done. Finally, when he was able to suppress any further thoughts of failure, he went right to sleep.

Although he'd had a bad night, Hebony was awake the next morning before the sun rose and went about the house gathering up the things he thought he might need. A small green cap to cover his head from the sun, a little bag of dry food, and some catnip. He would carry these in the little brown backpack his mother made for him. When the sky was bright, he said it was time to go.

There were a few clouds far out on the horizon that could kick up a sandstorm, but the odds of that were low. He found the mouse he had caught the night before and added it to the stash in his sack. He drank a whole dish of water, and with a well-wishing from his mother and siblings, he went to the bottom of a hill, said farewell to his littermates, rubbed his nose against his mother's nose, a cat goodbye.

As they parted, she called to him and said, "Watch out for wild animals. You don't want to end up being a jackal's supper." And Hebony started climbing up the steep trail to find out what was on the other side.

He started the trip by running up the hill at first and soon tired from the effort and from the lack of sleep the night before. He needed a rest, so he sat under the only bush he could find, and he was glad for its shade. When he recovered his strength, he decided he didn't need all the things he had been carrying.

The mouse he had stashed had already gone rancid, and he knew he could always catch another one when he needed to eat. He'd seen many mice scurrying around on the way up.

The hat made him look silly and might attract attention, so he threw it aside. *Cats don't usually wear hats*, he said to himself. *I could carry it along with me, but it could make a good nest for some bird, and my mother asked me not to litter up the trail.* And as for the catnip, well, he really didn't have time for that. He had a mission to go on. Hebony rested a little bit longer, and when he felt he was ready, he started up the hill again.

When he thought he must be near the top, he saw a flat area ahead of him. He hadn't noticed it from his view from home. As he entered it, a cold shivering wind blew down toward him, and it started to rain. The frigid air was flowing down from the top of the hill.

He didn't think it would be that cold in a desert, and he wished then he had thought to bring a coat or at least kept the hat he'd left behind. That would have kept his head warm. So to warm his body a little, he fluffed out his fur in order to keep the cold air further away from his body.

He had done this before because he knew it made him look twice as big as he was, and he'd done it to scare his littermates when they were playing. Now it made him feel warmer. But doing it also reminded him of the good times he'd had back home, and for the first time since he'd left home, he felt lonesome. But feeling warmer, even if he really wasn't, he continued on his journey uphill, and when he finally reached the top, the fog had lifted. He was tired, but he was rewarded by what he'd seen.

Looking down into the valley below, he could see what he thought might be the kitten mummification processing plant. The sun was setting, but using his golden eyes to pierce the thin gray fog that was beginning to shroud the hilltop again, he saw what he thought might be the buildings Horus had told them about.

There were many of them, but his eyes were drawn to the one that had the most activity going on outside of it. That building was longer than it was wide, and there were two large barn doors at each end.

Chariots, pulling wagons behind them, were going up and down the wide dirt road that led to the building, each pulled by a team of fine-looking horses and driven by bare-armed men dressed in leather pants and off-the-shoulder black leather jackets. Their golden-colored helmets glistened in the setting sun.

Great clouds of dirt spun up from under their wheels, and dust devils rose into the sky as they coursed back and forth over the only road he saw on the desert floor. As he watched, the sun began to set, and activity around the buildings slowed to a halt.

Hebony turned his eyes away and blinked. He knew he would have to wait until the next morning to go down the hill and try to get inside that building. So he walked to a clearing on the top of the hill and found a safe place to sleep in a dead end cave behind a pile of rocks, and he slept there until the next morning.

# CHAPTER 19

# Hebony's First Trip into Danger

The best way to face danger is to face it face on.

He slept well that night and spent the next morning studying the activity at the complex of buildings he had observed the day before. Then he walked along the ridge of the hill and searched for a trail that might lead him down to its base. He worked out several possible routes, kept some in mind, and others, he quickly discarded because they looked too steep.

By midday, his careful observations of the area below convinced him that there weren't any stray cats moving about down there, so he decided it wouldn't be wise for him to go down any of the trails during daylight. The "mingle with the stray cats" theory suggested by the gods wasn't going to work. He would have to go under the cover of darkness.

So that night, before the moon had come up, Hebony pussy footed down the hill on the path he thought would be the safest route. But he hadn't gone far before he tripped and almost fell. Then he wished he'd waited until the moon had come up before he'd started. But there wasn't any reason for him to hurry to the bottom. He had all night to get there.

So he sat down on a rock and waited until the moon was high in the sky and the path down the hill was well illuminated. Then he started down the path again, but even with the moon's light, he stumbled over rocks he failed to see.

When he finally reached the bottom, he walked toward the nearest building on the flat of his feet, and he kept his claws inside his paws so they wouldn't make any sound if they scraped on something. He was afraid that even the slightest little chirp made by a claw on a pebble would alert someone to his presence. When a dog barked in the distance, he stopped walking and listened for more barking.

When he heard none, he continued moving until he came close to the building. Then he bent his four legs forward so he could squat close to the ground and crept slowly with his tail near the ground until he reached a small window next to the barn doors. It was open a little at the bottom, but it didn't appear to be wide enough for him to crawl inside.

He squinted his eyes and ran a paw over them to remove some sand that had been blown by the desert wind. Then he jumped up on the windowsill and peeked into the room through the open space under the window's sash bar.

At first, he couldn't see anything, but when his eyes adjusted to the darkness, he made out something that looked like a large cage built of woven reeds. Then he heard the meowing of kittens, and he called to them in a soft voice.

"My name is Hebony. Don't be afraid. I am a friendly young cat here on a dangerous mission. Can you tell me what is going on in there?"

Everything was quiet for a minute or two. Then a tiny little voice answered.

"Well, I... Err... I don't know. I was told we were here for a purpose, but we don't know what that is. Each day a woman called Pakhet comes and takes a basket of us kittens away. She never brings them back. She just comes again and again to fetch more. We don't know what she does with them, and the fear of that makes us afraid. Have you come to solve this mystery?"

"Yes," Hebony replied. "I am going to do my very best to do that. I'm here to help you."

Then Hebony had a feeling he was being watched. He looked around but couldn't see anything nor anybody. A strong wind was blowing, and when a branch of a small bush brushed the nape of his neck, he almost jumped out of his skin, and he decided it was time to get away. He told the kittens that he'd had to leave before he was caught, and he told them he would come back to help them as soon as he could. Hebony left the building and carefully made his way to the bottom of the hill.

He wanted to learn more about what was going on in the building, but he didn't want his mission to end before it started, and he didn't want to be caught, and he surely didn't want to end up becoming a mummy himself.

He carefully scanned the perimeter once again, just to be sure he wasn't being followed, and he ran, tripping over stones and branches all the way to the top of the hill. When he reached the top, he was exhausted, and he sat on a rock to catch his breath as he watched the path below and listened for any sounds of footsteps.

When he thought it was safe, he laid down on the sand and catnapped. But he kept one eye open a slit to watch for someone who might have followed him. When he thought it was okay, he found the cave he slept in the night before, and he went into it again and slept throughout the long dark night.

# CHAPTER 20

# Down for a Second Look

Most everything requires a second look.

When the sun rose the next morning, he chased a mouse, caught it, and then remembered what his mother had said in one of her many lectures.

*"You should always eat the organs first. They have quick energy, and sometimes, you may not have the time to eat anything else."*

He butchered the mouse and ate the heart and all its other organs as he watched the activity at the building complex below.

When he finished eating all the organs that he had so carefully dissected from the mouse, he thought he'd eaten more than enough, so he tossed its remains, head, meat, skin, and tail, to a flock of blackbirds that had been watching him. Then he sat laughing out loud until his belly hurt as he watched them fight over each and every little morsel. So far, his trip had been very successful.

Then he turned around and fixed his eyes on the large building he had looked into the night before. It was a little past sunrise by then, and he saw that there was a lot of activity going on around it. Every now and then, a chariot would come up the road, turn in a driveway, stop in front of the barn's two doors, wait for them to be opened, and then be driven inside. He thought if he could get into one of the chariots unnoticed, he would be able to gain access to the inside of the building then jump out and have a look around during daylight.

But he would need to get from the cover of trees at the bottom of the hill to the edge of the road before he would be able to sneak into a passing chariot. He wasn't sure how he was going to do that. He had to go to the bottom of the hill again and make a plan there. Then he could learn what his options might be.

As he was watching the blackbirds flying overhead hoping for another mouse, a rainstorm came out of nowhere, and he huddled down and clung to a small bush until it passed. Then he got up, shook the rainwater out of his fur, hid his backpack in the cave so it would be there if he came back that way and started down the hill on the trail he'd come up the night before.

By the time he reached the end of the trail, the sun was high in the sky, so he hid in the cover of some bushes as he studied the open area that he would have to cross to reach the highway. The land was flat and sandy, but here and there, there were some short bushes that could hide him.

But, as he was scanning the area to plan a route, he was surprised to see some stray cats roaming among the bushes. So, he acted like he was just another stray cat and crossed to the edge of the road. The gods had been right after all. There were stray cats roaming around the complex.

He sat by the side of the road and watched as a line of chariots rode by. They would come speeding down the main highway, slowed down, and turn in the driveway. He thought it would be easy to jump into one when it was waiting in line, but if he did that, the driver might shoo him away. He didn't think they'd want cats inside the building. He'd have to get into a chariot when it was moving and the driver had his eyes on the road. There were small trees and bushes alongside the highway. So his plan was to find a tall bush or a small tree, climb up into its branches, and then when a chariot passed underneath, leap into it and hide under its seat.

He knew it was a dangerous thing to do, but if it worked, he would be able to get inside of the building unnoticed.

When he found a small leafy tree that he thought would do, he climbed up it and hid among its leafy branches and waited for the first chariot to pass by.

When a chariot came speeding toward the tree, its horses spouting hot breaths of air from their nostrils, Hebony hid from view within the heavy foliage on the tree, and as the rig passed by. Hebony was shaking from the experience, but he was not going to give up. He took control of his fears and waited patiently for the next chariot to come along.

He let the next two chariots slip by, and then he placed his feet firmly on the edge of the tree's largest branch and got into position to spring and pounce. And when the speeding vehicle came rushing by, he took a leap of faith and landed on the foot of the driver and then quickly ran under its seat. The driver, thinking it was only a rock he'd tossed up by a bump, shook his foot and drove to the barn doors that secured the building.

When the chariot stopped, a guard posted outside the building opened the doors, and the chariot went inside with Hebony safely hidden under the seat and well out of sight.

# Chapter 21

# Inside the Mysterious Building

You must get inside a problem in order to solve it.

Hebony waited as the driver spoke with some people and then stepped out of his two-wheeled cart and gave a gentle pat to each of his horses and walked away.

Hebony climbed out from under the seat and jumped unnoticed to the floor. Just then, a brown furry field mouse scurried from under a large earthenware jug. Hebony saw it and wanted to chase after it. He was hungry again, even though he'd just eaten the best parts of a mouse for breakfast, but he suppressed the urge and carefully crossed to the other side of the room. When he saw an open door that led to a room beyond, he knew he was in the right place because he could see the slightly opened window he'd spoken to the kittens through the night before.

Although the door to the room was wide open, he feared that someone would see him if he crossed to the room in daylight. Then he saw a small hole in the wall he thought might be a cat door for the resident cat, and he went to it. Then just to be sure the opening was wide enough for him to fit through, he carefully put his nose into the opening. His whiskers fit. It was large enough, and unseen by anyone, he slipped his whole body through the small hole and entered the room.

There was a small closet just inside the room, and he decided to hide himself up on its high shelf and wait there until nightfall. He hoped no one would open the door of the closet, but then, if they did, he surmised that anyone who did would think he was just a stray cat and chase him away. No problem, he could find another place to hide. In the meantime, he felt safe there. His guise of being just another stray cat seemed to be working, but he didn't want to push his luck. It wouldn't have been wise for him to go searching around in the daylight.

# CHAPTER 22

# The Search for Hard Evidence

Hard evidence is needed to learn the truth.

When night came and there were no more sounds of people, he jumped down from the shelf in the closet and listened for any other sounds in the room. Little kittens were crying somewhere nearby, and he slowly crept in the direction of their cries. When he found the first batch of kittens, they were quietly nursing their mother.

*Those aren't the ones crying*, he thought to himself, and then he whispered under his breath, "Oh my gosh. These people must be raising kittens to be mummified right here in this building."

He moved past the nursing kittens and went further into the room and came upon a large cage that held several young kittens.

Those were the ones that were crying.

"What is going on here?" Hebony whispered.

"Oh, we don't know," all the kittens replied all at once.

"We've only been here a short time. Maybe the sun god Ra crossed the sky two or three times. We don't know. We're so scared. What are you doing here? Are you the cat that was outside the window last night?"

"Yes, I am here on a mission to find the truth," Hebony said. "I want to make the world a better place for you. That's what I was born to do."

"We don't know what a mission is," one tiny kitten replied, "but we're glad you've come to make things better for us."

"We don't like being caged up," they all cried in unison.

"We want to run through the bushes and chase mice like other little kittens."

Hebony stood up and raised his paw to his lips to indicate silence and then whispered, "It looks like we need to make a plan. You all come near me now so we can come up with one."

Hebony was from the south of Egypt, and he spoke with a southern accent.

Then all the kittens came to the edge of the cage and cried, "Oh, what shall we do?"

"Well… Err," Hebony said. "We need to have a real good plan."

Then one of the kittens spoke up.

"I know, I know," the bravest kitten said. "When they come to feed us, we will all run out through the cage door and escape."

"Oh, yes. Oh yes, that's a good plan, a very good plan," Hebony said. "Okay, I'll hide nearby until feeding time, and when you are all safely out of the cage and running fast toward the door, I will follow you, and we will all run into the woods to plan our next move."

It wasn't long before a lady with a badge that read Aisha came into the room, carrying a large bowl of fish that had been imported from the Red Sea.

When she opened the door of the cage to feed the fish to them, all the kittens ran under her legs and tripped her up, and she fell to the floor covered with the slimy fish and salty water.

By the time she got to her feet again, all the kittens and Hebony had gone out through the door she had left opened and escaped into the woods. Later, they wished they'd eaten some of the spilled fish, but there hadn't been time.

# CHAPTER 23

# Into the Woods, Then What's Next?

Sometimes going into the woods is a good idea.

Once they were deep in the woods, they all stopped to rest.

"Now, huff, huff," a tired kitten said. "What are we going to do now?

Hebony needed to calm things down, so he said, "Well, when cats are nervous, they always wash their face just to make others think they aren't nervous. So take your front paws and wash your face."

Then they all washed their faces, even scrubbing behind their ears as Hebony sat down and tried hard to regain his composure.

After things had calmed down a little and every kitten had washed its face, Hebony told them he was going to try to find a mouse to eat. He hadn't eaten a good meal since he left home. So as he walked toward a patch of bushes to look for one, he turned around and advised the kittens to do the same, and every one of them scurried off into the bushes to find a mouse for themselves.

When they returned to the clearing, some had a mouse tail sticking from their mouth, others were sharing a slice of mouse butt ham with another kitten, and some were crying because they hadn't caught a mouse and they were still hungry. Hebony told them to share with one another, and soon they were dividing little bits of left-over mouse meat. After they'd all eaten their fill, every one of them, in cat fashion, cleaned its face, and then they all took a nap.

The next morning, they all woke up to the sound of chariots thundering down a rocky road nearby. The sound of beating of hooves on the hard pavement and the creaking of the ironclad wheels on the chariots filled them with fear. They hadn't noticed the road when they stopped to rest the night before. Now they were in danger of being found and returned to the building to face whatever was in store for them. Surely Aisha had told everyone about their escape. So Hebony rounded them up, and they all ran far away from the highway and into a secluded hamlet deep in the woods. Exhausted from their escape, they spent the rest of that day and that night napping and hiding among the trees.

Knowing not what he could do next, Hebony thought it would be nice if he taught the kittens how to climb up and down a tree. It was something he'd found hard to do. Maybe he could teach them a few tricks. So he climbed up into a small tree and fell down on his head on purpose. When the kittens rushed up to revive him, he quickly jumped up and chased them around the trees, and everybody had a good laugh.

Then he climbed up again and showed them how easy it was to go up and back down a tree as long as they kept their heads up. Then after a short nap, the kittens spent the rest of the day climbing, laughing, falling from small trees, and landing feet first in the deep piles of leaves that covered the floor of the forest.

That night, some wild cats they'd seen hanging around were invited to join them, and Hebony told stories and recited poems he knew would be written one day by the poet Edward Lear. All the kittens and the wild cats agreed that the best story was the one about an owl and a pussy cat.

The next morning when they woke up, the weather was bad. It had rained during the night, and everybody was wet. After they dried themselves, Hebony told the kittens he thought they were safe now because the people wouldn't be going up and down the highway in the rain. Then he led them through the woods until they came to what appeared to be a small settlement. It was time for him to leave these kittens and get back to work.

Hebony gathered them around him and told them he had completed their part of his mission and suggested they each go to the door of a nearby house and cry like a lost kitten. He said that most Egyptians were kind, and they would more than likely invite them in.

Then he went on to tell them that when they felt they were accepted, they should bring the people a dead mouse every now and then. If they did, the people would know they were useful, and they would have a home forever. The only thing that they must never do, he warned them, was to never suck their baby's breath away. None of them understood what he was talking about, but they thanked him for what he had done for them, and they went on their way.

# Chapter 24

# Back to the Mysterious Building Again

Sometimes you have to return to the scene of the crime.

Now Hebony needed to learn more about the place where the kittens had come from. He'd been able to get into the facility and save the lives of one cage full of kittens, but he didn't know for sure if the ones he saved would have been made into mummies or not. He had to get back into the building again and learn more about what was going on. He had a good idea he would find the answer there.

By the time he left the kittens, the rainstorm had ended, and the sun was high overhead. Being careful not to be seen, he traveled within the cover of the trees, and when he came to an opening, he quickly ran across it. At first, he didn't want to mingle with any other cats he met because his coat was black and he didn't want to stand out among them. He was on the mission again, and he wanted to reach the building before dark, before the doors were closed and he wouldn't be able to get inside.

When he found the road, he could see the mummy factory in the distance, and he followed the road until he was close by. No cat treated him like a stranger, so he took time to play with a few other cats he met, and an old woman was kind enough to give him a dish of milk. He drank the milk and thanked her by rubbing his flanks in and out between her legs. Then toward evening, he climbed a small tree alongside the side of the road and waited for a chariot to come by. Having mastered the skill of jumping into a chariot now, he leaped from a tree, landed on its seat, scurried under the driver's seat, and rode it into the building before dark.

Apparently, he had been able to catch the last chariot of the day. It was the only one left in the building. He waited as the driver unhitched the horses and took them out to the stable and closed the doors of the building behind him. Now he was safely inside the compound, and as far as he knew, he was alone. At first, he thought it would be a good time to look around the building some more, but then he decided it might not be such a good idea. He had no reason to push his luck. He already knew where he had to go.

So he found a large basket, hidden behind a desk, and he took a much-needed nap inside of it. When he awoke from his nap, it was late at night, so he got up and went directly to the room with the kitten cages. He remembered the way, and being careful not to wake anyone up, he walked right past the cages with mother cats with their kittens and crept up to the edge of a large cage filled with the older kittens.

He put his paw to the side of his mouth, emitted a little meow, and whispered, "Don't say anything out loud. I am here to solve a mystery and to help you. Do you know what's going on here?" he asked.

The bravest of the kittens, none of whom he had met before, called to him with a muted meow and told him the same story the other kittens told him on his first visit, and then they said, "There's an old lady with a limp in her leg. She must have fallen or something. Whatever it was, it happened a few days ago, but every day now, she still comes and takes a cage full of kittens away and never brings them back."

Hebony smiled when he heard about her limp. He knew what happened to her, and in his mind, he could see her lying on the floor covered with stinky slimy fish.

Now he knew he was on the right track, and the next thing he had to do was to find out what was going to happen next to these kittens. He told the kittens to be brave and to wait for his return. Then he went back past the nursing kittens to the basket he'd found and slept there until the next morning.

# CHAPTER 25

# What Was Happening in
# That Next Room?

Every journey into the unknown reveals something new.

When morning came, he could see that there was another large room down the hall, and seeing there was no one in sight, he walked boldly like a stray cat toward it. The room was brightly lighted by small grease burning lamps aided by rays of sunlight that came in through the many windows that lined its eastern wall. There were many wooden tables in the room, and men wearing white coats stood at each of them.

He jumped up on a high windowsill just inside the room, and by standing on his hind legs, he could see what was on top of the tables. Knives and other medical implements covered them, and there were lots of kittens' organs lying among them. He knew they were internal organs because they were the same shape and color as the organs of a mouse. Most cats wouldn't have noticed that, but Hebony had been a curious cat all his life, and long ago, when his mother had brought him a mouse to eat, she found him studying its innards before he had eaten them. She was the one who had told him that they were the most nutritious part of all animals and that he should always eat them first.

Of course, his mother didn't know what to call each organ, but when she pointed at the heart, she told him that was the best part to eat.

Each table held many small round clay Coptic pots on top of them, and the men were carefully putting the little organs from each kitten into each of them. He didn't see any hearts, and at the time, he wondered where they were. Women dressed in colorful lab coats came into the room from time to time and picked up the pots and carried them out through a wide doorway that led to a walled courtyard. Now Hebony needed to know what was happening out there.

So he quietly jumped down from the windowsill, and not making a sound or being noticed, he landed near the opening. When he got outside, he found that he needed to get high above the ground in order to see what was going on. But it was dangerous for him to be out in the open. If the women saw him, they might treat him like a stray cat and chase him away with a broom. But up high above the ground, he would have a safe vantage point where he could watch what was going on and not be seen. So he climbed to the top of a tree, and from there, he watched the activity below and listened carefully to hear what was being said.

Hebony hadn't been around people very much before the trip, but his mother had taught him a few of the words the people spoke, so he was able to understand a little of their conversation. Their chatter was about embalming or something like that, and as he watched, the woman dug holes in the sand and buried the clay pots in them.

Then they went to the other end of the courtyard and dug up pots that were already buried there and carried them to a long table where they removed kitten's organs from each pot and put them inside of what looked like the body of a furry little kitten.

The contents from each pot filled a single kitten. Then these pots were taken to another table where women dressed in blue coats wrapped them in layers of brown Egyptian cloth and packed them side by side in wooden boxes. Now he knew that these were the kitten mummies the rumor was about.

(There were no hearts in the pots during the process of embalming because the heart was never removed from the body. They believed the heart was the center of thought and necessary to salvation after death, and it was always left in the body of the deceased to ensure its availability at judgment and during the afterlife.)

Now Hebony had all the evidence he needed to know about the mummification facility. The kittens were being raised there and were mummified there. Now he needed to learn where the mummies went from there, and he needed to find a way to follow the boxed mummies to their final destination. But before he would do that, he had some unfinished business back inside the building.

# Chapter 26

# Searching for the Final Piece of the Puzzle

No puzzle can be finished if you're missing a piece.

He went back to the room where the cages were filled with cats and kittens were and opened each one of them. He let all of them out and told them to scurry away into the streets and try to find a home with a kind person. Then he went outside and walked toward the road that ran behind the building. When he saw a lot of activity going on out there, he climbed up into a nearby tree so he could see what was going on. Parked at the curb below him were many horse-drawn chariots.

Each one of them had a small wagon hitched behind it. Women dressed in brightly colored dresses were carrying wooden boxes filled with cloth-wrapped kittens to the wagons and placing them in neat rows two boxes high. When a wagon was filled to its limits, the driver spoke to the horses, and the chariot turned away from the curb, gained speed, and was soon far out of sight.

Hebony climbed down from his vantage point in the tree and walked slowly along the street and jumped up on top of a hitching post near the wagons, and when the people turned their backs, he leaped into a wagon that was half-filled with boxes of mummies and hid in an empty covered box at the front of the wagon. There were some old rags in the box, so he curled up on top of them and waited until the wagon was filled. When the chariot left the curb and turned into the road, Hebony was hidden inside the box, and he was off to its unknown destination.

The dirt road it traveled turned out to be filled with ruts and bumps, and Hebony had to dig his claws deep into the wood floor of the box in order to stay under the seat. He didn't want the driver to see him if he were to be tossed into the bed of the wagon with the boxes of kittens.

But there wasn't much chance of the driver looking back into the bed of the wagon. He was too busy navigating his way around the moguls. But soon the pavement smoothed out, and Hebony was able to remove his claws from the wood floor and enjoy the rest of the ride as he watched the passing scenery through the narrow openings between the boards on each side of the wagon and through some tiny cracks in the board on the top of the box, then he sat back, relaxed, as he watched the rows of trees and buildings along the road as he passed by them. When, just by chance, he happened to look up through an opening in the box, he saw a fancy sign hanging above the road. Of course, he wasn't able to read what was painted on it, but it told the ones that could read that they were entering the City of Alexandria.

Alexandria was a fine city at the time, and Hebony watched its landmarks as the chariot sped along its hundred-foot wide well-paved streets and past gleaming limestone colonnades, temples, beautiful palaces, and a towering white lighthouse far out in the harbor. And behind the harbor was an expanse of blue water. Of course, Hebony didn't know what a lighthouse was, but its gleaming white tower had caught his eye, and it made such an impression on him that he knew he had to find it and climb to its top before he went home. Soon, the rig arrived in the middle of the city, and it finally came to rest at the marketplace and parked under a large trade sign covered with pictures of little cat mummies. The sign identified the building as the Mummy Store. Hebony remained hidden beneath the wagon's seat until the wagon was unloaded and the driver had walked away.

Then he jumped to the pavement and stood on a bench that was in the shade of a small tree. Its shade and a gusty breeze coming up from the sea cooled him from his hot ride under the wagon's seat.

When he looked around, he couldn't believe what he was seeing. There were salesmen selling kitten mummies. Some of the men were dressed in robes. Most of the mummies were wrapped in brown cloth like the ones he'd seen being wrapped at the factory, but there were others that were much more elaborate. Those were wrapped with gold leaf and had precious gemstones set into their head as eyes. Hebony thought the people were buying a mummy to take home for their own use, but most of the people were taking their mummy up a path that led to the top of the nearby hill.

# CHAPTER 27

# There Is Another Hill to Climb

His journey might be over.

Hebony had learned the truth about the rumor. It was true. Kittens were being killed, and now he knew why. They were being killed to be made into mummies, taken to the city, and carried up a path that led to the top of a hill.

Hebony jumped down from the bench and followed the people who were climbing up the hill. When he reached the top of the hill, he found himself in the midst of a large festival. Clouds of smoke filled the air with an aroma of flowers and spices. Loud music was playing, and there were people who were kissing, hugging, and bumping against one another. Others danced in the streets or staggered around as they drank from large silver cups that had pointed bottoms, which made them impossible to set down until they were empty. The people who had carried a mummy with them hurried to a temple, bowed at an elaborate altar, and touched their forehead as they placed the mummy on the altar, kneeled, and spoke quiet words to them. Most of the time, this was a somber event, but every now and then, a person would place a very special kitten on the altar, one whose body glittered in the sunlight and bore eyes that sparkled like lightning. Then somber thoughts and remorse were over, and the most beautiful woman he'd seen held the kitten over her head and danced in circles as the people cheered. Basset, Basset, Superstar.

Hebony felt sorry for the little kittens that had been killed for a gift to the gods, and he muttered to himself, "Killing a cat is a crime even if it is a gift to a goddess. Nobody should be above the law."

He looked to the ground and shook his head from side to side in sorrow as he walked back to the path that led down the hill.

That day should have been a day of joy and satisfaction for Hebony, a day of closure and celebration. The day, he could have started home and have said, "Mom, mission accomplished."

But the events he'd witnessed at the top of the hill that day saddened him. He knew very little about the worship of the gods. He was too young to understand such a mysterious concept. His mother had told him he was being sent by the gods to learn the truth about the rumor, and now he'd just witnessed a ceremony at an altar where the cat goddess was accepting mummified kittens wrapped in golden cloth and studded with precious jewels. His mission was over. He'd done his very best, and he had learned the truth. But now he was sad.

And now, after all he'd been through, he didn't know if he wanted to go home and tell everyone how bad the truth was. He thought it might be better to let them think he had been eaten by a jackal. In time, they would forget him, and interest in the rumor would die out.

When he left home, there was no hard evidence that anything evil was going on. The rumor may have just been that, something the gods made up. Gods were known for playing tricks on the people. Maybe it was a diversion from the more important matters they had to deal with.

But he had seen the raw truth of it all with his own eyes, and it was hard for even him to process what he had experienced that afternoon. He took one last look at the trail of white smoke rising up from the festival grounds, and as he walked down from the hill, he remembered the aroma of flowers. The scent of the flowers was the only thing there that had pleased him.

# CHAPTER 28

# A Visit to the City of Alexandria

A visit to a city might educate you.

When Hebony came back to the place where the mummified kittens were unloaded from the wagons, the crowds were gone, and all the wagons were empty. A small group of chariot drivers were seated on the bench under the shade tree. He guessed they were relaxing and counting their wages. He quietly went past them unnoticed and made his way to a street that ran toward the waterfront, a street he thought might lead him to a lighthouse he'd only caught a quick glimpse of when he was hiding inside the box in the wagon.

He thought he might never have another chance to see anything so beautiful as that lighthouse again, and he needed some kind of diversion to wipe the despair and sorrow that filled his heart. As he walked further down the street, his mind filled with doubt, he decided he would spend a few days in Alexandria before he made up his mind about going back home. That thought made him a little happier, and then he was able to put his troubles aside. Uplifted, he stopped walking and began to run along the street that ran toward the sea.

Then he quickly crossed to another street and then another, and he didn't stop running until he noticed a small number of cats in a park, and he slowed to a slow trot. He wanted to sneak past them. He didn't know what the local cats might do to an interloper, and he was in no mood for trouble. But an orange tabby saw him sneaking by and called to him.

"Hi, stranger. I haven't seen you around these parts before. Where are you from?"

Hebony stopped walking.

"I live over that far hill," he replied, pointing the way toward his home. "I don't know any name for the place, but it's where I was born."

Hebony continued to walk down the street as he answered. He wished he could stop and play. He hadn't done that since he left home, and he missed having fun. But he just wasn't in the mood for merriment right then.

The orange tabby followed him down the street in a friendly manner, but he soon gave up the chase and called out to him again.

"Well, okay, stranger, welcome to Alexandria. We come here almost every afternoon about this time. I guess you must have other things to do. We'd like to get to know you. We don't see many strangers around here."

When Hebony reached the edge of the water, at the Palace Harbor in the Port of Alexandria, he noticed some strange little red crabs running sideways on the wet sand. He wasn't sure what they were, so he carefully placed his paw on one, and the creature snapped up its upturned claw and nipped him on his toe. Hebony shook his paw and jumped back onto the grass. He thought they might be some type of scorpion he'd never seen before, so he left them alone and went on his way along the water front.

Then he was surprised when he heard a man in a small boat call to him.

"Hey, Mr. Cat, would you like a fish? I've got some fresh herring I caught today. Come on board."

His mother told Hebony long ago that he had the ability to understand the language of the people, but this was one of the first times he had experienced it. Hebony fully understood the fisherman's words, and he leaped onto the deck of the boat, walked along the gunnel, and jumped into its little cubby cabin.

Not only had he hardly ever been spoken to by a human before, it was the first time he'd seen a boat, and he almost lost his balance when it rocked as the waves hit the shore.

"You need to get your sea legs, Mr. Cat," the man said as he placed a dish of fish on the deck.

Hebony didn't know how to eat fish, so he slapped at the lot of them with his front paw to see if the strange things were dead or alive. He didn't want to be nipped again. The man laughed and recognized his problem and picked up one of the fish and cut it into smaller pieces. Hebony sniffed the small bits of fish and ate some. He liked the taste of fish, but he left a little on the plate.

"Eat up, kitty," the man said. "You look like you could use a good meal."

Hebony ate a few more pieces of fish and left the rest behind. He'd been used to sharing his food with the other members of his family.

"You sure are a strange cat," the man said. "Would you like to go out to sea with me?" They say black cats bring a fisherman good luck when they go to sea with them."

Hebony didn't understand what the man was talking about. He'd never seen the sea before, so he didn't respond.

Besides, he wanted to get to the lighthouse before dark, and the sun indicated that the day was more than half over. He went to the fisherman's legs and weaved his body in and out between them. He thought that might be a good way for him to say thanks. Then he leaped back to shore and ignored another colony of the little red crabs that ran sideways on the sand, and he went off again in the direction of the lighthouse.

# CHAPTER 29

# A Little Romance

We all need a little romance in our life.

When he reached a wide boulevard that came down from the city and joined the street that ran along the waterfront, Hebony decided to stay on the street he was on, and he continued his way toward the lighthouse. He still thought he would make it there that day. But then he noticed a sweet fragrance of flowers in the air. The odor was similar to that of the flowers that bloomed on the magnolia tree that grew behind the house where he was born. That big old tree that he and his siblings practiced climbing skills when they were kittens. But when he found the magnolia tree, there were no blossoms. Then he thought that maybe the sweetened air came from the white Egyptian rosebush, a plant he was told to stay away from when he was a kitten because it had needle-sharp thorns that could hurt him.

But still not sure which plant it was, he searched around the vegetation looking for a flower that might help him remember. But then a tiny voice called to him, and he looked up and saw a small female tabby cat sitting on an ornate wooden bench.

"Hello, are you new here?" she said. "I haven't seen you before. I always come here to sit on this bench in the afternoon to warm my fur. I love the color of your coat. I've never seen a coat that color before. "Would you like to come and sit next to me?"

Hebony was unsure. He had never been asked that question before. He wanted to see the lighthouse, but he had plenty of time, and he knew it would still be there later in the day. So he walked over and jumped up on the bench and sat next to the tabby. He was nervous. He'd never spoken to a female cat. He didn't know what to say. But then he felt braver.

"My name is Hebony," he said, puffing out his fur and trying to sound like he'd said this many times before. "This is my first time in a city. I live just over that big hill over there. What's... Err, what's your name?" he stuttered.

"I'm Khari," the tabby replied.

"Khari," Hebony said. "Why, that's the name of my sister. I have a sister and two brothers."

He moved closer to the tabby, and the fragrance in the air grew stronger. Then Hebony, trying to act grown-up again but not knowing what to say again, said, "Do you notice the aroma of flowers?"

"Yes," the tabby said, "it's coming from that bush over there. I think it's a rosebush of some kind."

"Oh, that's the white Egyptian rose," Hebony replied in an effort that he thought would impress her. "They grow near my home. I guess you know they have sharp needles that can hurt you?"

The tabby shook her head to signal yes and then began to purr.

Hebony responded by moving closer to her, and they sat together and made small talk until the sun began to set.

Then Khari asked, "Would you like to come home with me? I haven't had my lunch yet. I usually eat about now, but I sort of lost track of time when we were talking. You're a very interesting fellow. I know it's a little late in the day, but aren't you hungry?"

"I had a few fish when I was down near the seashore," Hebony said. "A fisherman gave me some, but I can always eat a little more. Yes, I guess I am hungry."

The two of them jumped down from the bench and walked side by side along the foot of the many streets that led up the hill toward the city of Alexandria. When they passed the fisherman Hebony met that afternoon, the fisherman called to Hebony. "Looks like you made a friend today. Good for you. We all need friends. Say, if you two have a little time to spare, come over here and sit with me on this park bench. It's close to sunset, and I think there might to be a rare sight out in the sea this evening. The weather is just right for it. It's called the flash of green."

Hebony and Khari walked over and sat on the bench next to the fisherman, and he told them, "Just as the sun goes down beneath the horizon, you may see a quick flash of the color green just above the spot where the sun went down."

The three of them sat waiting for the sunset without saying a word, their eyes moving up and down and side by side to avoid being blinded by the power of its light. Then, just as the sun dispersed beneath the horizon, the fisherman said, "There it is! There it is! Did you see it? Did you see it? If you did, you've seen a rare sight."

"I didn't see anything," Hebony muttered. He was thinking that he might have been hoodwinked by the fisherman.

Khari sat head down, moving it from side to side. Then she looked up and said, "I noticed a quick movement as the sun dipped under the water, but there was no flash of color."

"You have to be quick," the fisherman replied. "You have to keep looking at the water just under the sun, not into the sun. That could blind you. And you can't even blink your eyes. Well, better luck next time."

*The flash was there. The fisherman saw it, but what he didn't know was that all cats are said to be colorblind.* Hebony thanked the fisherman for asking them to stop by, and then he and Khari jumped from the bench and walked in the twilight until they came to a small white house surrounded by flower gardens.

"I live here under the house," Khari said. "It's just a small place, but it's dry and out of the rain. I feel safe here. There's a dog that lives upstairs. We get along okay. He's my protection." Then she laughed. "Oh, he won't hurt you. He's a good old dog."

Then they went through a small opening in the foundation and sat together on the dirt floor.

"It isn't much," Khari said, "but it's home for me now. I'd like to get out of the city someday. Where was it you said you lived? I might like it there."

Hebony didn't know what to say. They talked some more as they shared some dry mouse jerky Khari had taken down from a floor joist above them. After they'd eaten, they laid down together on the dirt floor and fell asleep. Khari woke up first and nuzzled Hebony's chin with her nose and asked if he would like to spend the night with her.

But Hebony said quickly replied, "No."

He wanted to get to the lighthouse before dark. He wasn't ready for a relationship. He had to go home with some news about his mission. So they sat together with one another a little longer, each thinking what to say or do next, and by the time Hebony went outside to walk to the lighthouse, it was dark.

"It's not safe to be outside in the dark," Khari said. "We may be living in the city, but at night, the jackals come here to hunt. You better stay here for the night."

Hebony turned around and came back inside. They finished the leftover jerky and sat looking at each other again. Khari arched her back, swished her tail, and then laid down close beside him and made little cries and rolled over and over on the dirt floor. Hebony didn't know what she was doing.

"Please, Khari," Hebony said. "I don't know what you're doing. What is the matter with you? I hope you're not going to be sick."

Khari stopped what she was doing and went outside.

When she returned, Hebony said he was very sleepy, and he went over and laid down on the other side of the room. But when he woke up the next morning, Khari was sleeping next to him. He carefully got up and stood next to her and spent a long time watching her as she slept. He was moved by the beauty of her body, and he reached down and ran his paw lightly at her back, taking care not to wake her.

Then he whispered a silent goodbye up into the air and went out into the dim light of the morning. He had a compelling urge to stay with her, but duty called. He had his mission. He had to decide what he should do about it.

Then with one last look at Khari, he caught his breath and went out through the hole in the foundation and into the nearby garden. He caught a mouse there that wasn't quite awake and left it in her doorway along with a fallen blossom from the white Egyptian rose-bush he'd found.

Then as he left, he paused, turned around, and spoke toward her in a voice so low that it wouldn't wake her, "Maybe I'll come back someday, and we can visit the lighthouse together. One never knows what the future may bring."

# CHAPTER 30

# A Visit to the Lighthouse

If it's there, and you have time, visit what you can when you can.

When Hebony reached the base of the lighthouse, the memory of Khari still haunted him. He thought of going back but suppressed the impulse and started up the many steps that wound around in the steep spiral stairway to its very top. When he reached the top, he was out of breath. He rested a few minutes and then jumped up to the high shelf that circled the wall just under the windows. He was 450 feet above the ground in what was then the tallest building in the known world. As he walked around the promenade, he could watch the activity going on in the city below, and he could see far out to sea. There were many ships and boats in the harbor that day.

Some were coming in or going out of the inlet. Colorful square sails on the boats added many pale colors to the sparkling blue water of the harbor as did the shore birds and Ibis as they slipped their beaks into the shallow water and green grass in search of their last meal before the sun was high. The boats that were anchored rocked and swayed with the cadence of each wave. Hebony watched the boats for a long time as he wondered if he would ever want to go to sea in the fisherman's boat. Then he thought to himself he might not. He didn't think he'd like to be on anything that rocked all the time, and he knew he couldn't go to sea or anywhere else until he decided what to do about the killing of little kittens.

He went back down the steps and went into the street and began to walk up the paved road that he hoped would lead him to the mummy factory. He was still not sure if he could go home with the news or not. So he went on up the road. He would have to make up his mind when he arrived home. He knew if he didn't go home, his mother would always worry about him and he couldn't do that to her. He wondered if he should lie to her, but when he thought about it, he knew he had to tell her the truth. He would think of a way to just tell her the facts and leave out the ugly things he'd seen. He would spare her of that. Today, he would just follow the road and think about it. At any rate, the mission was over and done...or so he thought.

# CHAPTER 31

# The Chariot Race or
# Why Are People So Competitive?

When Hebony found a road that he thought might lead him back to the mummy factory, he noticed at once that the one he'd found was filled with bumps and ruts, and that reminded him of the country road he'd traveled along when he rode under the seat of a wagon filled with mummified kittens. Sure now that he was on the right road, he sprinted along it, hoping he wouldn't be run over by a speeding chariot.

When he noticed clouds of dust coming up from a ring of rocks just off the highway, he slowed down, trotted off the highway, and went through some tall grass and then jumped up on top of one of the rocks that surrounded the dust cloud. There he found some local cats watching a large number of horse-drawn chariots speeding around in a circle.

Hebony greeted them, told them his name, and asked what was going on.

"It's a chariot race," one of them answered. "It's part of the festival. Brave men drive their chariots around in a circle to see who has the fastest one. It's fun to watch. Sometimes there are wrecks, and their chariots fly up into the air, and the drivers and their horses get hurt. Then the race is stopped, and people come out and drag the injured men off to that grassy area just outside the track. Women in white coats come to see if anyone was hurt, and if there are, they treat their wounds. Sometimes the driver dies."

"Why do they do it?" Hebony asked.

"Because they are competitive," said a bull's-eye tabby named Grosso. "Each one of them wants to win the race and prove that they're the fastest chariot driver. It's the same with all the people. No matter what they're doing, they all want to be the best. They seem to enjoy the competition."

Then an orange long-haired cat who called himself Ringo stood up, arched its back, looked at Hebony, and added, "Yes, I agree. It seems to be a silly trait that all the people have."

Hebony shook his head from side to side and replied, "What do they get if they are the fastest and they win the race?"

"Oh, women put flowers around their neck, and then they're awarded a shiny gold or silver cup they can keep. That shows everyone they won the race. They just get silly things like that."

"Do cats ever compete with one another?" Hebony asked. "I've never been in a city before, and I never heard that word before. Competition seems silly to me. I'm glad I'm not a person. I wouldn't want to have to risk my life to show that I was better than any other cat. I think I'd rather cooperate with other cats than compete with them. I thought all cats would feel that way."

Just then, two chariots spun off the track, and the discussion about competition ended as the chariots rolled and over and over until one of them landed on the grass right in front of them. The local cats scrambled back toward the road, but Hebony crept closer to examine the wreckage. Both chariots were broken into pieces. The one nearest him was laying on its side.

A wheel that was still attached to the wreckage was spinning slowly in the air as Hebony approached it. The wheel from the other side had flown off and was bouncing up and down through the tall grass as it made its way toward a group of spectators on the other side of the track. The driver was lying on his back and was crying out for help.

But Hebony didn't know what he could do to help him, so he crossed the track to examine the wreckage of the other chariot. He was beginning to think that watching chariot racing might be exciting until he noticed that the driver's head was missing from his body. He wondered where it was, but he chose not to look for it.

When he thought he'd seen enough of the carnage, more than enough, he walked back toward the other cats, told them what had happened, and said he thought the race was over because of the accident.

"I guess they didn't have any winner for that race," the orange tabby cat said.

"Sometimes the races end that way, but there'll be another one next year. We don't understand why they race either, but it's fun to watch the people make fools of themselves."

Hebony bid them goodbye and continued on his way. He wanted to make it to the mummy factory before dark. When he reached it, he would make up his mind about going home or not.

# CHAPTER 32

# Hebony Makes a Cat Friend

One can never have too many friends

But Hebony hadn't gone far down the road toward the mummy factory when he noticed that the large bulls-eye tabby cat named Grosso, whom he'd met at the races, was following him. Hebony stopped walking and waited for him to catch up with him. When Grosso stopped next to him and he caught his breath, he said, "Hebony, that is your name, isn't it? I think you better come home with me tonight. There are jackals out in the woods at night, and they sometimes hunt near the roads. I don't want you to be eaten by one of them. you seem like a nice guy. I'd like to get to know you better. Will you stay with me for the night? The people I live with have a little house down the road. They're nice people. They wouldn't mind."

Hebony thought about it. He had been a little worried about spending the night alone, so he followed the tabby cat to the house. After they shared a bowl of meat and camel milk, they went to the room where Grosso slept. He showed Hebony where he slept and pointed to a pillow on the other side of the room. Hebony jumped up on the pillow. He thought it would be okay, and then he walked over and sat alongside Grosso. When he did, Grosso stood up and said, "Hebony, I followed you this evening because I wanted to talk to you about something you said today when we were watching the race. You seemed to be saying that you thought that competition was silly. I think you said that you thought racers shouldn't risk their lives competing to see who's the best. I'd like to know if there is anything you would risk your life for."

Hebony sat silent as he mulled over the question. He had been risking his life to learn why the kittens were being killed and made into mummies. He would have to say yes. But until that night, he hadn't thought about his mission that way. Then he spoke.

"Maybe I shouldn't have used the word risk and competition in the same sentence. I should have said I thought that anyone who would risk their lives to win a trophy was silly. Only a crazy person would do that. I think these people really do it just to satisfy their ego. Winning a shiny cup does nothing to help anybody else, nor does it make life any better for anyone. But in answer to your question, I do think there are some things worth risking your life for. You never asked why I was at the race today, and I never thought to tell you. I think we were all too engrossed in watching the race. I've been risking my life for the past few weeks by going on a mission to learn why some people were killing little kittens and making them into mummies. I had a few close calls. I almost fell out of a tree when I was trying to jump into a fast-moving chariot." He didn't elaborate. "But I think I've found the answer, and now I'm on my way home to report what I learned. But I didn't think much about risks until now. All I was told when I left home was to watch out for jackals. Thinking about the risks I've taken since then makes the fur on the back of my neck stand up."

Then Hebony thought of another way to say it.

"Grosso," he said, "come to think of it, I don't think risk and competition are the same things. We all take risks. I'll be at risk until I end my mission, but I'm not competing with anyone else by doing it. I don't think cats ever compete with one another. We're all individuals. We get along with one another. We mingle and play with each other, but we don't compete to find out which one of us is the best. We don't hunt together in a group or keep count of who catches the most mice. Wolves and dogs hunt together in packs and are always competing with one another to see who will become the next leader of the pack. Gazelles and Nubian ibex live together in herds, and horses and camels would do the same if they had the chance. But cats are loners. We come together for social reasons and speak a common language, but we don't hang out together all the time.

"I'm a guest in your house right now, but even if I lived next door, we wouldn't do this every night. Maybe we don't compete because we don't need to. I don't think cats care who's the best. We see one another as equals. I think people may be the only ones that compete with one another?

"I've never watched a race before. But do you think the horses in that race today wanted to compete with one another? I think, if they had the choice, they'd rather have been out in the pasture eating grass. My guess is the people made them do it. If I were a horse, I would fight back. I wouldn't run in any kind of a race nor would I pull people around in a chariot or help them till their crops unless I wanted to. I would guess that way back when, the people must have tried to enslave us too. But I think that to a cat, we stuck together and refused to be enslaved. It is something all the other animals should have done.

"Man should not have dominion over the animals. They should all be the master of their own destiny. They should have expressed their right to be free. I think the people believe that they were given dominion over the other animals. Well, I think each animal has the right to control its own destiny. Those animals should have stuck to their ways, just like the cats, gotten up and walked away. Sometimes nonviolence is the only way to preserve your freedom and not become someone's slave. The horse should have resisted until the people found another way to pull a wagon. Did you know that the people and some tiny little jungle ants are the only animals that make slaves of their own kind? Well, they didn't make slaves of us cats, and I'm ready to take on anybody that wants to make a slave of me!

"Gee, Grosso. I don't know where I learned all that. It just came to me out of the blue. Mom was right. I am not an ordinary cat. Wow, that was some speech I just made. I'm sorry. I had to get that off my chest. Let me go on now. A cat could never be tamed and made to enter a race. Oh, we might do a few tricks to please the people, but only if we wanted to. We came to live with them out of our own free will. We didn't come into the cities because there were people there. My mother said, we came for the mice. We get along with the people now that we're together, but they don't own us. We could go back and live in the wild anytime we wanted to. Do you know why some people don't let their pet cats out at night? I think it's because they love them and they're afraid they'd run away."

With that, Hebony asked Grosso where he should go to the bathroom.

"Oh, just go anywhere in the yard," Grosso said. "I'm not allowed to do it in the house."

Hebony went out to the yard and did his business very quickly because he thought he heard jackals yipping. When he came back in from the yard, he sat down and spoke to Grosso again.

"Now I think there might be some good reasons to risk your life, but only if you do it because you think the outcome will make things better. As I said before, racing to win a silver cup seems silly, but taking a risk that could make life better for others could be a risk worth taking. It's the purpose and the outcome that matters. I think we should always do things that make things better than we found them."

Grosso excused himself and said he had to go outside to check on a mouse hole he'd been watching, but Hebony knew he really had to go to the bathroom, so he chose not to tag along.

# Chapter 33

# Hebony Learns Some Manners

Always mind your manners.

As Hebony sat alone in their bedroom, waiting for Grosso to return from checking out the mouse hole, a veil of lonesomeness came over him, and he began to reminisce about the few friends he had back home. Until now, there hadn't been much time for him to think about anything else; but now that his mission was almost over, he wanted to relax and just have a little conversation. So when Grosso came in from the yard, Hebony asked him to come over and sit next to him. Grosso mumbled something about the mouse not being anywhere near his hole, and then he wandered over and eased down on his haunches. When you got down on your haunches, you lowered yourself toward the ground so your legs were bent under you and you were balancing on your feet. This position was usually used by a sick cat, but Grosso wasn't sick. He sat that way just because he liked doing it every now and then.

When Hebony saw Grosso sitting on his haunches, he wanted to laugh because he thought he looked funny sitting that way. But then he thought it might upset him, so he just smiled and looked Grosso in the eye and said, "Grosso, I think we have a lot in common. I wasn't born knowing all those little facts of life. I think a lot of what I know came from our mother. I think I told you that I have a sister and two brothers. Well, she was always telling us kittens about the things she thought we needed to know about when we grew up. But I was more than surprised the day she told us that she was afraid that the people were destroying the land and that good, fertile land was something we all needed to save to go on living here. My mother knew a lot about the land and what was being done to it by the people. Well, this revelation fired up my curiosity, and it drove me to want to know more about the people, how their attitudes on life differed from ours, and just what the people had been doing to destroy the land. I've been searching for answers ever since. Until I met you, I'd never met another cat that seemed to be aware that the people were doing things that cats would never do, like competing with one another to be the best at whatever it was or risking their lives and limbs to win a race. You seem to be a very educated cat. Where did you learn all that you know?"

Grosso looked up and replied, "Hebony, knowledge comes with age. The longer we live and the more cats and people we meet, the more things we know. Then when you add in all the things you've learned for yourself, you know a lot more than you know now. But that's only if you pay attention. I wish the people would look around and see what they are doing to the land. If they did, they might notice that what they were doing was wrong and change their ways. But I think most people have their heads buried in the sand. If they didn't have their heads buried in the sand, they would be able to look around them and see that what they are doing was wrong, and then they might be able to change their ways before it was too late. This may be the only land there is. Nobody really knows how much land there is, and if the people ruin the land and they all die, there would be no grain or leaky grain storage towers. Then the mice would move back to the desert, and we'd have to learn to hunt wild mice again. That would be a bummer. And what about the cats that are living with the people? Some of them have become used to drinking warm camel milk, and they may have forgotten how to catch mice. Sometimes I wish the people still lived in caves. Life was harder then, but cats lived on the land for a long time before the people came. Oh well, we can't do much about the people because we don't have opposable thumbs as they do. If we did, we could take over what was left and build cities of our own."

Then Grosso rocked back on his haunches and thought about what he had just said. Then he spurted out, almost laughing when he said it, "Oh no, what was I saying? "I don't think we want opposable thumbs." As the saying goes, power is addictive. There is no end to what cats would do with opposable thumbs, and I'm not going to speculate about it. I'm sorry about that. I got carried away. Cats don't need to build cities to be happy. We lived off the land without cities for a long time. Maybe I should lay off drinking the juice from fermented fruit. The other day, I found a date tree out by the water hole, and I drank some rotten date juice, and now I'm a little tipsy. So let me start our conversation over again. I think you started this discussion with me when you said that I was an educated cat. I do know a lot more about the people and about all the foolish things they do, but now you've made me think about the people in a different way. I never questioned why the people competed with one another all the time or why they always wanted to be the best and how they abused other animals to show how good they were. Things like that didn't bother me then, but they do now. Stick with me, Hebony, and I think we will become good friends."

Hebony said he would like that, but then he butted in, "Before we discuss that any further, I have a question I'd like to ask of you. It's something I've been wondering about ever since I met you." Hebony hadn't discussed any touchy subjects with other cats except the ones he'd grown up with, and when he asked Grosso the question, it showed his lack of good manners. "Grosso," he asked, "why do people call you Grosso? I never heard a name like that before."

What he said to Grosso might sound trivial to you, but it was something he should have known better than to have asked a friend he hadn't gotten to know very well. Grosso was a very fat cat, not in a way that meant he was very rich. It was because he was very much overweight, and Hebony should have thought about that before he spoke. But Grosso wasn't upset. A lot of other cats had asked him that same question before, and he knew the reason why. "It's because I'm overweight," Grosso answered. "My real name is Ramses. Grosso is my nickname. They call me Grosso because I'm fat. But I don't know why I'm so fat. I don't eat that much. I just can't help it. But being this big slows me down. That's why I was out of breath when I caught up with you on the road today, but I don't mind being asked again. It's something I've had to live with all my life."

Even though Hebony hadn't learned his manners, he knew by then that he'd said something wrong, and he tried to make it right. "Oh, I can understand that, Grosso. I'm so sorry I put it that way. I should have known better. I used to be called bad names when I stuttered when I was trying to say some words. Sometimes the other cats teased me about it, but I'm better now. I hope you can find some way to lose some of your extra weight. Can we talk a little more about c-c-c-competition now?" Hebony stuttered because he was nervous. "I know what the word *competition* means, but I don't understand why the people are always competing with one another."

Grosso thought a little and then replied, "Oh, it's like I told you before. It's because they get a prize when they win a race. People always cheer for the winner. Losers don't get many cheers. When you compete and win, you're the one the people cheer about, and they call you a hero. I guess I'd have to say that the people race as much for the cheers as they do for the silver cup. The people seem to need praise from other people to be happy, and the silver cup reminds everybody that they won that race. It's a lack of self-worth, and most people, it seems, don't have very much of that. You need to believe in yourself and you should be happy when you accomplish something, but you don't need to rub it in. That just makes the losers feel bad. I think it *would* be better if the person who won the race would offer to help the losers do better the next time they raced. Cooperation would be better than competition. People should race for the fun of it. There always will be winners and losers. Everybody can't win. I'm glad cats don't have to compete with one another to be happy. Cats don't compete with one another, and I don't think the cats will ever let the people put one of them into a harness, make us pull a wagon, or run in their races. If they try, they'll be sorry." He didn't elaborate.

Hebony sat silent, then he replied, "I don't think I'd like to have a lot of noise made over me." "I didn't get to hear any of the cheering at the end of that race today because of the wreck. The noise was bad enough during the race. I'm glad I wasn't watching a race when somebody won. Loud noises hurt my ears. Have you ever heard of anything cats do to compete with one another?"

"Well," Grosso said, "male cats compete over females. You'll learn about that when you're older. And cats that live with people compete for their affection. When there's more than one cat in the house, each cat will compete hard to get attention, and a cat will compete with a dog if one lives in the same house. I guess all animals would compete for food if they're hungry enough. But there is something else I don't understand about people. It is why they all need to be better than one another to be happy. I think cats are born happy."

Then Hebony spoke again, "I didn't know much about competition until now. Maybe that's why I'm happy. But I wasn't happy the time I fell out of a tree when I was being taught how to climb one. I could never seem to remember that I had to climb up and down a tree tailfirst."

Grosso had a good laugh, and then he said, "I don't even try to climb trees anymore. There's no future in it.

Then Hebony replied in little more than a whisper, "But, Grosso, come to think of it, would you say that I was competing with myself when I was learning to climb up and down trees? Every time I fell out of one, I got mad at myself, and I climbed right back up and tied it again. I wasn't going to let any stupid old tree get the best of me. But my mother told me that, that was okay. She said I was just being persistent, and being persistent was something that might help me out someday. Do you think persistence is competing with yourself?"

Grosso yawed, arched his back to relax his muscles, and said he thought being persistent was a good thing, and then he suggested they should both go to sleep, but Hebony wanted to ask another question, and this question was about something Grosso had spoken about a few minutes before.

"Grosso," Hebony said, "you told me that cats compete for females, and you said that I would understand why when I was older. Can you tell me now? Just tell me cat to cat. I can take it. I think I'm old enough."

Grosso stood up, walked to the other side of the room, shook his head, and then came back and sat next to Hebony again. He'd never been asked that question before, and he didn't quite know what to say. So he raised a paw and washed his face as he searched for an answer. "It's about making kittens, Hebony," Grosso finally said. "Male cats mate with female cats to make them have kittens. When your time comes, you'll understand. I don't really know how to explain it to you now, but when it happens to you, if you are ready for it, you will want to stay very close to a certain female cat, and you may compete with other male cats to keep them away from her. Then you mate with her, and that's it. It happens and it's over before you know it. Then you each go your separate ways and you may never see one another again. Mating is something that all animals must do in order for life to go on. We all grow old and die, and without mating, there would be no offspring born to take our place. Mating is necessary for all animals. They all want to produce offspring that will be just like or be better than themselves, so they compete in order to pass on these traits to their offspring. I guess that's a good thing, but it doesn't always turn out the way they wanted it to. Sometimes offspring have a mind of their own. But my gosh, Hebony, I thought all mother cats told their kittens about mating. I don't remember where I learned about it, but I've known about it for a long time. It's something all male cats have to do. Without mating, there would be no more kittens."

Hebony stood up, arched his back, and whispered, "I think that's what happened to me when I was in Alexandria the other day. I met a female cat on a park bench, and she invited me to spend the night with her so I wouldn't be eaten by the jackals. She was the first female cat I was that close to. But later that night, when we were lying together on the floor trying to go to sleep, she reached over and stroked my fur, and then she started purring and rolling around on the floor next to me. I didn't know what she was doing. So, I didn't let her know that I was still awake. Then she stopped purring, and I think she fell asleep. When I woke up the next morning, she was still asleep, and I left to go to the lighthouse before she woke up. Do you think she wanted to mate?"

"I guess so," Grosso answered. "You'll understand all about that when you're older."

Well, they talked late into the night, and they didn't go to sleep until they agreed that taking risks that made life better for others was worth taking and that winning just to please yourself was foolish and selfish, and then they went to their beds.

But Hebony couldn't get to sleep. His mind was spinning. One part of his brain wanted him to join Grosso and sleep, but another part of his brain was hungry for more knowledge. So he got up and walked around the room, thinking about what he should do. He knew he had to leave for home in the morning. There were people at home who might be able to make his risky trip worth taking, but there were things he needed to talk to Grosso about before he left. He hated to wake Grosso up, but Hebony knew he would never be able to get to sleep with so many unanswered questions on his mind. So he walked over to Grosso and tapped him on the shoulder.

When Grosso opened one eye, Hebony said, "I hate to wake you up, but there are so many more things I want to discuss with you before I have to go home. Can we talk just a little bit longer?"

Grosso opened his other eye, yawned, and then muttered to himself, "Young cats, young cats, why did I ever invite a young cat into my life, especially one with an unquenchable thirst for knowledge?" Then he stood up and rubbed his eyes. "Hebony, don't you ever want to sleep? You have a long journey ahead of you in the morning. You need to get some rest. The night must be more than half over by now. Can't this wait until morning?"

Hebony apologized and he felt remorse again as he whispered "I just need a little time Grosso. I promise." After we talk, I'll stay asleep until you wake me up. I promise. I cross my heart and hope to die.

Grosso was the first friend Hebony had ever made, and now he was beginning to see Grosso as the father figure he never had. He respected Grosso, and he wanted to learn more things about life from him, things that a father cat should teach his sons. As Hebony thought more about that, his mind wandered back to his age-old question: Why do male cats always leave the raising of their kittens to the mother cat? He wanted answers to that question and to the long list of other questions he already put on his mental list of the things he wanted to teach his kittens when he had kittens of his own.

The role that male cats played in raising their kittens was something Hebony had been concerned about since the day his mother told him that all male cats always left the raising of their kittens to the mother cat. That was the day he upset her when he told her that he wanted to change that age-old tradition and help his mother cat raise their kittens when he had kittens of his own.

When Grosso finally got out of bed and stood next to Hebony, Hebony fidgeted, excused himself, and said he had to go to the bathroom. He then asked Grosso if he thought it was safe for him to go out in the yard alone.

Grosso yawned again and said, with a little bit of frustration in his voice, "Hebony, it's never safe to go out in the yard. Nothing is 100 percent safe. If you have to poop, you don't need to take time to bury it. Do it near a bush where people won't step in it. The people that live here curse their dog when they step on his poop. Don't be like a dog. Okay?"

Then in an effort to stay awake until Hebony came back into the room, Grosso washed his face, the top of his head, and then he rolled over on his back and reached his head down washed his belly.

When Hebony came up from the yard, he was still half asleep, and he was mumbling something about what he was going to teach his kittens when he had kittens of his own. He didn't know what to teach his kittens when they grew up, and he knew nothing about the needs of female kittens, and he was about to ask Grosso about it when Grosso said, "I heard your mumbling, Hebony. That's what mother cats are for. Let her teach them. Mother cats teach kittens to be kind and to love one another. You may be able to teach your male kittens to think your way about the things you want them to know. But most male cats, like most male people, will teach their male offspring to be the spitting image of themselves and to be ready to fight off any potbellied, baggy-eyed bully who wanted to boss them around. Let the mother cat teach them everything. Mothers have to go through the pain of childbirth. They know what pain and suffering are all about. Our mothers teach us a sense of love and caring for each other. Without a mother's advice, we all would be at war with everybody all of the time. We should thank the gods for mother cats and for the little female kittens that follow her advice when they have kittens of their own."

When they both sat down in the middle of the room again, Grosso yawned again and said, "Okay, now what was so important that you had to wake me up in the middle of the night?"

"Okay, okay, okay, don't have a tizzy," Hebony replied. "Before you went to sleep, you and I were talking about the men who won the races, and you said that when a person won a race, the people cheered and called him a hero. I'm still not sure what a hero is. Could a person be called a hero for doing something other than winning a race? I just need a quick answer. And what about the horse? Is a horse ever called a hero?"

Grosso didn't answer right away. Then he replied, "Yes, sometimes the horse is referred to as a hero, but all it gets is a bucket of grain to eat. The word *hero* has been used to describe many things. But since meeting you, I've come to think more and more, that just winning a race shouldn't make anyone into a hero. Lots of people win races. Maybe it would be better if the term hero was only used to honor those who accomplished something they chose to do because they thought that by doing it, they would be able to change things for the better. Or maybe that honor should be reserved only for those who, on the spur of the moment, takes a risk that goes beyond the call of duty and they go off and do it and save a life. I'd call you a hero because you risked your life to save the lives of little kittens that you don't even know. You accepted a dangerous mission. You faced the dangers, and now you're going home to finish what you started, and you've even come back with more than you were asked. Even if you were eaten by a jackal, you have accomplished what no other cat had ever done before. You should be proud of yourself. We need more cats like you."

When Grosso noted that Hebony was dozing off, he poked him with his paw and said, "Hey, little buddy, don't fall asleep on me now. You're the one that wanted to talk in the middle of the night. You woke me up when I was having a good dream. I was just about to catch the biggest mouse I'd ever seen. He was this big." Grosso spread his front arms wide as he would if he were a fisherman describing the fish, he'd caught the other day. "Now I'll never know how my dream would have ended. You owe me a mouse. A big one. Now sit up and listen to me. We both need to get a good night's sleep, and if we don't finish this discussion before morning, I may forget what I've already said and repeat something I've said before. So listen to me. I'm not a history buff or a hero worshiper, but I've heard the people who own this house talk about the heroes they've known about. The male person in this house is a teacher of some kind, and he invites some of his favorite students to come over in the evenings and talk about heroes. I like to lie on the floor and listen to them. They discuss men like Nectanebo and Thutmose and a female hero named Hatshepsut. These were all pharaohs.

"One night, a long time ago, they were talking about the people who won at the games. They thought that some people might have been born with a rare skill they didn't know they had until they found it by chance. Say, a boy is born with a hidden talent for throwing the javelin. Unless he has a chance to throw a javelin, he would never know he had that skill. But if somebody gave him a javelin and he threw one for a great distance the first time he tried, it's likely he would be told to try out for the games. And if he won at the games, the people would more than likely call him a hero. But then the question was, was he born with a rare skill, or did he win because he threw it very well? Some said yes, and others said no. Some people said he won because only because he was a natural who was born with the skill. Others said that he won because he practiced a lot. You told me that your mother said that you were born with the skills you needed to complete your mission. I think that maybe we are all born with some unique skill, but then we have to find it in order to apply it, will do some good. The sad thing is that most unique skills are only discovered by chance and some may never be found.

And that's because the person born with the rare skill has to be at found at the right time and in the right place. For example, the boy who was handed a javelin and won at the games may never have known that he had that skill unless someone had handed him one. So

I'm not sure whether I should call you a hero because you were born as a natural to go on such a mission or because you worked hard to complete something that you wanted to do because you though that, in the end, it would help other little kittens.

Either way, I think you will be called a hero when you reach your goal and complete your mission. But it sure would have been a lot less work for you if you were a natural and you were born with the skills you needed. But don't stop working. You may not be a natural, and you still have a long way to go before your mission is over.

Then Grosso, who was still sitting on the side of his bed, decided to change the subject; and he got up and stood on the bedroom floor for a long time. Then, he fixed his eyes on a large knot that protruded from one of the floorboards, and he walked around the knot in small circles as looked at Hebony. He addressed him; and with much lament in his voice, he said, "Heroes, heroes, heroes Hebony."

There were so many kinds of people those students' called their heroes. Some of them had taken chances with their lives and worked hard to complete something that would have qualified them to be called a hero. But some others were generals who led their armies into great wars during which many people were killed on both sides. War is such a nasty business. But these generals didn't care much about the numbers of people who would be killed in these wars. They used propaganda to convince their soldiers that all their enemies were evil, and they ordered them to kill them—combatants and civilians alike.

And when the battle was over, there were many deaths on both sides. Those were mothers' fathers, sons, daughters, and pets who would all be mourned long after the war was over. I'll guess I'll never understand why the people are always going to war or why they are always building more armies to prevent more wars in the future. Their wars never solved anything. The only ones who benefited from them were the ones who made money building the weapons of war and the undertakers who buried the dead. The history of the people is written on their battlefields.

The people should take a clue from the cats and learn how to get along with one another. My mother didn't teach me to hate other cats just because they were of another breed from another country or were a different color. She told me that I was expected to get along with all the other cats, the people, and all the other animals I met, even if one happened to be the dog that lived in our house.

She said that no matter where mother cats may mate, they never teach their kittens to hate. It's something the people ought to teach to their children. They need to accept other people as they are and learn to get along with them. Those other people had no choice as to where they were born. They have a right to be proud of who they are. If all the people did this, it would make life better for everyone in the land. The people need to end the hate within themselves. Hating one another just leads to more hate, more wars, and more suffering and death. I wouldn't want to stay here in this house if the people downstairs were always fighting. I'd be afraid they might kick me around just because I was a cat. Some people don't like cats. We love the people. We came into town to help them control the mice, didn't we? Well, maybe not. My mother said we came here for the mice, but we didn't have to like the people to do that. I like the people in this house, and I think they like me. There is no sense in hating anybody else. It just makes you sad. I wish there was a way to make the people stop hating one another. But later that night, one of those students spoke about the heroes who built great cities like Alexandria and won wars. I guess there are all kinds of heroes. If I were a person, I might want to build a city or go to war too, but I'm not a person. I'm happy just being a cat. People could learn a lot about living if they studied the ways of cats. Cats seem to be satisfied living just the way things are. They never built cities, fought wars, changed the land, or diverted rivers to suit themselves.

"Maybe life would be better if cats ruled the land again. I think we should all stop wanting to be called a hero for every little thing we do. We should always do our very best, no matter what it is, and let it go at that. You shouldn't have to be the winner to be happy. It's only a race. Just run your race with friends and treasure the time you spend with them. Racing doesn't have to be about winning or losing. Good friends are more valuable than a trophy. We can talk more about what makes a real hero the next time we get together. I think there are so many heroes now that the people have diluted the value of the word. It seems it's too easy to become called a hero. But then I'm not a person and I'm speaking like a cat again. Cats never expect to be called a hero for catching lots of mice, but it would be nice if a cat that rescued her kittens from a fire be called a hero or the cat that wakes a person who was asleep in bed when there was a fire in their house. It takes a real hero to risk his, or her, life to save the life of another."

But by this time, Hebony was sleepy, and he was paying little attention to Grosso's long speech. Then out of the blue, he said, "What is a javelin?"

Grosso ignored his question. He wasn't sure how to explain what a javelin was. Then he said, "Please go to bed, Hebony, and go to sleep, I'll tell you in the morning."

*****

They woke up early the next morning, and the thing about the javelin never came up. They shared a bowl of camel's milk and went to the porch and sat together on its top step. They sat silent for a moment and stared down the old dirt road that led from Grosso's home and then faded into fields and woodlands that seemed to go on forever. Neither of them said anything for a long time. Then Grosso spoke with a bit of sadness in his voice, "Well, it's about time for you to start going home, Hebony. It has been nice talking with you. I'm glad we met. I'm going to miss you." And then in a lighter voice, he went on to say, "But before you go, I've got a joke for you."

Hebony looked at Grosso. "What is a joke?" he replied.

Grosso smiled and said, "It's something to make you laugh. Here it is. How do you catch a mouse that's hiding down in his hole?"

Hebony looked at Grosso and smiled at him but said nothing. So Grosso went on. "Well, there's a plant that grows out in the desert that has little round berries hanging from its branches. The people call them peas. So what you do is you put a ring of peas around the mouse hole, and then you hide nearby. When the mouse comes up from his hole to take a pea, you pounce on him."

Hebony looked at Grosso. "I don't get it," he said softly.

"When he takes a pea, Hebony," Grosso replied, raising his voice, "when he takes a *pee*. When he goes to the bathroom, see? That's the joke, Hebony!"

Hebony smiled and said, "Okay, I still don't get it, but thanks for asking me. I'll need to think about it."

Grosso smiled and said, "Hebony, you've got a lot to learn, but now you'd better get a move on. The sun's up. The jackals should be sleeping by now. You better be on your way."

When Hebony stood up to leave, he remembered something Grosso had said to him the night before. "We can talk more about what makes a real hero the next time we get together." Now he took that statement to mean that he was welcome to come back again, and Hebony said to himself, "That's it. I'll go home now and come back another time and talk with my good friend, Grosso." Hebony had made a good friend. He puffed out his fur and made himself look much larger than he really was. He was very happy. He ran down the front steps, two at a time, and started home, thinking about the day when he would come back again and talk with his old friend.

# CHAPTER 34

# But then Hebony Had Some Second Thoughts

Sometimes we change our mind.

Hebony hadn't gone far before he began to think that it wouldn't be wise for him to go past the mummy factory during daylight. At first, he was mad at himself for not thinking about it sooner. If he had, he could have had more time with Grosso. But then he thought that Grosso might have had other plans, and he didn't want to infringe any plans Grosso might have made, so he took his time and spent the day walking through the woods, studying the wildflowers and thinking about the little female tabby cat he'd met in Alexandria.

He thought the encounter with her was over, but every time he found an Egyptian rosebush or inhaled its sweet aroma, he thought of her again. But as the day passed and evening came, the memory of her faded, and a primal fear of the oncoming night engulfed him. He knew it was time for the jackals to wake up. So he stopped searching for wildflowers and hurried through the woods toward the road that would lead him to the mummy factory. There, he thought he would find safety by sleeping high up in a tree.

# CHAPTER 35

# Hebony Comes to a Crossroads of Life

At some time, we will all find ourselves at a
crossroads and wonder which road to take.

But it was late in the afternoon when he arrived at the place where
the road that led from the bull's-eye tabby's house and the main
highway that would take him to the mummy factory or the City of
Alexandria, so he sat at the crossroads and thought about what he
wanted to do for the rest of his life. Then that intersection became
more than an intersection of two highways. It became a crossroads
for his future. Once he had been just a little country cat.

But now he'd had a taste of city life, and he began to think
about all the exciting things going on in Alexandria, things he would
never be able to experience again if he went back home. He thought
about what his mother told him about the choices he would have if
he grew up there. None of those would satisfy him now. He didn't
want to be a mouser in the streets, just a cat that made more kittens
or be somebody's house cat.

He'd been exposed to what could be a much better life for him
if he stayed in the city. If he lived there, he could become the black
cat that would make the fisherman's boat lucky, or maybe he and
Khari might be able to get together and make lots of kittens that he
could help her raise.

Then he thought about what he'd told Grosso just the night before. At that time, he thought his mission was almost over and that all he had to do then was to go home and report his findings. His mind had been made up then. Then he thought again about the day he had traveled down the crossroad road that went to his left. That was the day he'd traveled it hidden in a cart filled with little mummified kittens.

At that time, his only thoughts were to learn where the kittens were being taken and what would happen to them when they arrived. He had been sure then that it would be the final chapter of his mission. But now the memory of his time in Alexandria made him think about changing his mind again. He mulled over which road he should take. If he went left, it would take him past the mummy factory and over the hill to home. The road to the left would take him to Alexandria and to the wonders of a whole new life.

He sat at the crossroads watching the chariots race by. Some of them were towing wagons. He wondered which ones were carrying mummified kittens.

He thought about the priests in Alexandria who were selling cat mummies to the masses. They had soured his mind on the values of humanity. The incident at the temple where the people were giving the little cat mummies to their gods disgusted him, and he began to wonder what the meaning of life was all about in a big city.

A certain part of his mind urged him to abandon his mission altogether and never go home. Little demons of the mind asked him the questions like what would he do if he went home to report his findings and nobody was there? Or what if no one who was there believed him? What would he do if his mother wasn't there? Would anyone else listen to him?

Then his own thoughts turned to the many choices he would have if he stayed in the city, and he mulled over each of them. The fisherman had offered to take him out fishing, and then there was Khari, the cute little female cat he had met in the park. He was fairly certain that either one of them would invite him to stay with them if he asked. He liked the thought of that.

But then he thought again and wondered if choosing either of them would really be a good idea. The fishing trip was very tempting. Hebony had acquired a taste for adventure on his mission, and now he was craving for more. Facing and overcoming danger had sparked excitement within him. But he didn't think he wanted to go out fishing to find it.

He thought about Khari again and wondered if she could become his next purpose in life. He needed a new purpose now that he had fulfilled the one the gods had given him. But then he thought he couldn't go back to her. Maybe he could learn to love her, but he wasn't really ready for that kind of love, even if it meant he could be a real father to their kittens, a father that would stay at home with her and help her raise them, and then he wondered if he was really ready to be a stay-at-home dad.

# CHAPTER 36

# Hebony Finally Decides
# What He Will Do

Choices in life must be made by you.

But when Hebony's thoughts came to the realization that he had made a commitment to return home when his mission was over, everything fell into place. He had to go home. He had to honor his commitment. He could always come back to Alexandria; it was just over the hill from where he lived. He didn't have to stay at home forever. Besides, his mother told him that she would soon be leaving him. And as for his brothers and sister, they would have to go their own way as soon as they were old enough. Then he decided that he wasn't committed to staying on that side of the mountain.

He was committed to honor the promise he's made to his mother and Annipe. So Hebony banished the negative thoughts from his mind and took the left fork of the road.

That fork would lead him to the mummy factory and to a trail he would follow as he made his way back home.

# CHAPTER 37

# Hebony Meets a Stranger

Be open minded, the stranger you meet might change your life.

Hebony hurried along that road. It wasn't dark yet, but he knew he needed to find a safe place to spend the night. As he walked along that road, he searched for a tree to climb, one that was too high for a jackal to reach him, then he saw an old man standing by the side of the road, and without such as a thought or a meow, he ran to him and weaved his body through and around the old man's legs.

"Well, hello, cat," the old man said. "Where did you come from? It looks like you're one of those weaving cats. Will you please stop weaving in and out between my legs? You could trip an old man doing that. We don't see many cats around here, and a black one like you is a rare sight indeed. I've heard there were black cats like you, but I understand that most of them never grew up to be your age. Black isn't a good color for a cat, especially when they live in a white sandy environment like the desert. People tell me it's the jackals that eat most of them. I guess you're one of the lucky ones."

Hebony shuddered at the thought of being eaten.

The man reached down and petted the top of his head. Hebony liked that. He was tired, and he thought the man's gesture was kind and inviting. Then without any resistance from Hebony, the man put his arms around him and picked him up and carried him through the dense woods to a small grassy clearing. Hebony had gone to sleep on the way, and he woke up then only because the man stopped walking. He was upset because he had slept so deeply cradled in the arms of a stranger.

That wasn't catlike at all, and he was mad at himself for having let it happen.

But then he excused himself when he began to remember the very busy time he'd had during the past few days, and he muddled over them in his mind.

The incident at the temple on the hill, time spent wondering if he should go home, a day in Alexandria, his first time on a boat, meeting what may have been his first love and leaving her behind, climbing to the top of a lighthouse and viewing the possibilities he could have had if he stayed there, watching a chariot race, spending a night with a new friend, discussing the meaning of things through that night, a day of walking through fields of wildflowers and facing the crossroad of his life.

It was more than any mind should have to deal with. He wanted to go to sleep, but he didn't want to fall asleep in the old man's arms again. He relaxed a little and stopped thinking about the past and looked at the woodlands around him. There was a little white house in the middle of the clearing. It was surrounded by old twisted trees. Some of them towered over it.

Gnarly armlike branches missing most of their bark reached down and scraped, like a carpenter's chisel, on its roof top. An old coat of dirty-white paint and a sagging porch made the house look older and more dilapidated than it really may have been, and he wondered if he dared to go inside. Then when he looked away from the house and searched the yard, he became mad at himself all over again, and he thought to himself, *I should have searched the yard before I took so darn much time examining the house. One of those little jackals, the man warned me about, might have been waiting for me in the bushes. Sure, I was tired, but that was no excuse.*

After he carefully searched the yard and found no signs of danger, he squirmed and jumped to the ground and sat in the yard with his back to the old man, thinking about what he should do. He thought of running back through the forest by the way he had come, but then he wasn't sure which way that was.

But before he could make up his mind, the old man looked down at him and said, "Evening has come, Mr. Cat. The desert out there can be hot during the day, but it becomes very cold at night. You better come inside this old house and spend the night with me. It will be nice and warm in there tonight."

Hebony agreed, turned, and walked toward him, but as he did a wave of fear came over him, and he began to wonder if this man might have been sent by the priests to catch him and take him to jail. Maybe this man was the one he thought he'd heard spying on him the first night he'd gone down the hill to spy on the mummy factory. He felt sure that there was something or somebody there besides him. It could have been a guard; this old man could have been that guard.

He wasn't wearing a gown now, but neither were some of the priests who were selling kitten mummies to the people in Alexandria. He felt he might be in danger, and for the second time that day, he had a strong urge to run back to the road where he had met the man and find a tree to climb. A tree that was so high nobody would be able to see him hiding in its branches. He knew he could run faster than the old man, but he still didn't know which way to run.

So he sat down and watched the old man walk ahead of him. Then he came up with a plan. He would follow him into the house and try to win him over. He had no other choice.

He had to trust the old man or face a forest filled with jackals that might eat him. He was between the devil and the deep blue sea.

Hebony followed the old man up to the porch, walked up its four rotten steps, and waited as he opened a large squeaky wooden door that barred their entrance. Hebony was hesitant to enter his house at first, but a gentile push with the side of the old man's boot propelled him inside, and as the squeaking door closed behind him, its rusty hinges cried out even louder as their eerie sound ricocheted off the walls and sent icy cold shivers up and down his spine.

This time, he made it his business to carefully explore the interior of the house before he did anything else.

It was easy. There was only one room sparsely furnished with a weathered wooden table and a large log bench. A small open fireplace stood at its far wall, its embers turned to ash. When he was satisfied that the room was safe, he went around sniffing the floor for any scent of mice. He was hungry.

Then he sat on his haunches and watched as the man took some wood from a small basket and started the fire in the fireplace. He'd never seen a fire before, and the dancing of its flames fascinated him. The man stood with his back to the fire for a long time to warm himself then turned around and said, "I'll bet you're hungry. There's not much to eat around here but some dried fish I brought back from the docks the other day. Do you like fish?" Without waiting for an answer, he went to a small cabinet hanging on the wall, opened it, and took out two dried fish. He put one in his mouth then reached down, broke the other one into little pieces, and offered them to Hebony.

When Hebony finished the meager meal, he jumped up on the log bench, curled up, and went into a light-sleep mode, the sleep mode cats use to nap until they feel safe enough for deep sleep. In light-sleep mode, a cat's eyes are opened just a slit, both ears are wide open, and their whole body is energized and ready for fight or flight.

Hebony needed rest, but he had to be sure he was safe. He still knew nothing about this man, but he had to trust him. Besides, the man had already closed the heavy door when they came in, and there were no windows. He had no other choice, and he went into a deeper sleep, but he knew, like all cats do, that he would be awakened by the slightest sound. House cats are small when compared to the other animals they live with, and their light-sleep mode has helped them survive.

# Chapter 38

# The History Lesson

History tells you the thing that happen before
so you don't repeat them again.

As Hebony slept, the old man did a little house cleaning. He swept the ashes in front of the fireplace, straightened a picture that hung on the wall near the fireplace, and then came and stood by the bench where Hebony was sleeping. He watched Hebony's ribs rise and fall with each breath then, being careful not to disturb him, and he sat down alongside him. He wanted to pet Hebony, but he didn't want to wake him.

Instead, he stood staring at the old picture that hung on the wall near the fireplace. Flickering flames from the fire made it almost impossible to see its image, but he knew who it was. It was his wife, who had died many years ago. Looking at her picture always brought back fond memories of the happy time they had together when she was alive.

Then, as he listened to the sounds of the crackling fire and Hebony's purring, he began to reminisce about his past. He had come from a long line of low-level priests. During the years he and his wife had been married, they had three sons. Two of them had been killed in battles, and their youngest son had returned from war, so scarred from the things he had to do to win his battles that he couldn't talk to anybody about them, and he had gone to live far away, and they lost contact with him years ago. Many of the old man's friend and buddies had served in the military too, and many of them had died, and he was glad that he'd been a priest and hadn't been called to duty. But he'd have gone if he had been called but not to kill others. He would have aided the wounded and prayed for the dead and asked the gods to bring an end to the war before any more people were injured or died. He saw no sense in wars. They'd never really solved anything. He said there was always another war. He said that he thought it was a serious fault in the minds of the people.

And as he looked down at Hebony, he remembered a certain battle his forefathers told him about long, long ago.

It was the Battle of the Persian Conquest, one of the many battles that had led to the beginning of the end of the Egyptian empire. In that battle, a man named Cambyses, who, with the help of the Bedouins, nomadic Arabs, led his army across the miles of desert to reach an Egyptian outpost. Cambyses was aware that the Egyptians worshipped cats, and he'd brought cages filled with captive cats to release into the battle. The Egyptians might well have won the battle at the outpost had it not been for their love of cats. Because when they saw all the cats their opponent had brought, they feared the cats would be harmed by the fighting, and they threw down their weapons and lost the battle.

The old man knew a lot about cats. He loved them, and he thought about keeping Hebony as his pet. Then, again being careful, not to wake Hebony, he laid down on the bench and went to sleep next to him.

Neither of them stirred until the fire burned down, and the room became colder. The chill awoke the old man, and he got up to rekindle the fire. He added some wood and stoked the ashes until the fire burned bright. Then he stood with his back toward the flames to warm his body. Then, not remembering Hebony was there, he started speaking to himself out loud. It was something he'd always done. Speaking out loud is something many lonesome people do. It makes them feel better, even though they are well aware that there's no one there to hear them. Their mind supplies them with answers that mysteriously come from someone they wished was there in person.

# CHAPTER 39

# A Surprise for Hebony

A surprise comes as a shock.

Hebony had been sleeping sound at the time, but he was awakened when the man began to speak so loudly. Until then, the man had spoken to him in a softer voice, and Hebony had understood him and responded to his suggestions and commands. But this time, the tone and the volume of his voice were different, and he felt even more compelled to listen. He sat up and cocked his ears toward the old man and looked into his face. It was an old, weathered face wrinkled with age, but it was a kind face.

Hebony laid down again, made himself more comfortable, cocked his ears up again, and listened to what the old man was saying.

His accent was harder to understand when the man spoke so loudly, but Hebony was still able to understand every word he said, and somehow, he knew that the man was speaking to him, and he was very surprised when he spoke about the mummy factory.

He told Hebony that he had once been a priest, not a high priest but a low-level priest who served a higher priest.

"My first assignment," he said, "was working at the local cat mummy factory just up the road from here. I wasn't involved with the killing. I was an inspector in one of the many rooms where the embalming was done. At first, I thought I was helping the people and doing them a service by providing them with mummified kittens to

116

please their gods. I was involved with quality control, and my job was to make sure that the organs, all but the heart, were removed from each kitten and were dried and then returned to that same kitten before it was wrapped in linen.

"The heart was never removed because it was thought to have something to do with the soul and it's coming back to live in the afterlife. But as time went by, I felt differently. It didn't seem right to me that people should be sacrificing kittens to please anyone, even a god. These kittens were just little innocent animals who knew nothing of gods or of worship."

He paused, speaking long enough to recheck the fire and then came over to sit down next to Hebony and went on speaking. He was sure that Hebony was listening to him now, but something told him he was telling Hebony things he wanted to know.

"One day," he said very loudly, "I had enough. I just walked away. I didn't quit. I just walked away, and I didn't look back. Something told me it was the right thing to do. During my wandering, I found this old fishing shack. It was filled with nets and floats and hooks and poles, the things fishermen use. There was nobody living here, so I moved in. I've been here for nine years. It's not much, but it's my home now."

Hebony had been very surprised when he first heard the man speak about the mummy factory. He hadn't expected that because there was no way the man could have known what his mission was. So he laid still and continued to listen because he wanted to be able to bring home as much information about the mummy factory as he could.

The old man spoke on telling him about the clergy and the priests and priestesses of Egypt and what their other duties were.

"The clergy," he said, "didn't preach, interpret scripture, proselytize, or conduct services. Their job is to take care of the god in their temple. High priests worked full-time and made a good living, and their jobs were usually passed down from father to son. The lower-level ones, like I had been, worked part-time, helping a high priest on busy days and at their large festivals. Both men and women could serve the clergy. They performed the same functions and received equal pay. Enough to get by, but not really enough to live on. Women were more often priestesses serving female deities while men served the male deities."

The old man stopped talking again and went to tend the fire. Then he went outside to relieve himself. Hebony followed him and squatted in the grass as the old man waited nearby.

"Better be quick, Mr. Cat," he said. "People tell me there are jackals around here at night. You'd make a good meal for one if it caught you."

Hebony quickly finished his business and didn't take time to bury what he had done. Then he quickly followed the old man back inside, and they both made sure the door was shut tight. As they checked the fire together, Hebony became interested in the flames, and he reached one of his paws toward them. The old man saw it and nudged Hebony with his foot and said no, and Hebony pulled his paw away, and Hebony went back to the bench. The old man remained by the fireplace. Resting his arm on the mantel, he began to speak again.

"Some priests were satisfied with their lot in life," he said. "Some were not. They were the ones who wanted more. Most priests, high or low, worked part-time at other jobs as well as the clergy. They worked in the villages alongside common people and mid-level bureaucrats. These were the people who put new ideas into the priest's heads. It was some of these unhappy underpaid priests who started the mummy factory. They opened it because they thought making cat mummies would earn them a lot of money.

"Things were going bad in Egypt back then. Long after the Persian conquest, Alexander the Great invaded their land, and everything changed. Then the invasions of the Greeks and Romans followed, and they made even more changes. And because of them, the people thought their gods had forsaken them. They thought that maybe the gods wanted more from them. Then somebody came up with the idea of making mummified kittens and selling them to people who would buy them and take them to the gods as an offering. Basset was their major god. She was the cat god.

"So these clergymen became corrupt and opened and operated the cat mummy factory. They bred cats there, and they made mummies from their kittens. Then they sold the mummies to people who bought them to offer to their goddess Basset, hoping she could bring the good times back. Sales were so good that the factory had a hard time keeping up with the demand, and now the priests were making all the money they'd expected to make. At times, like during fiesta, the workers spent day and night working to meet their quota."

The old man stood up then and shouted.

"The whole darn system went corrupt, and it still goes on today. These are sad times, my young fellow, very sad times."

Then he walked across the room and petted Hebony and repeated in a lower voice, "It's sad, my little friend. It's so sad."

When Hebony looked up into the old man's face, he saw a tear run down his cheek, and he looked away so as not to embarrass him. He thought he had learned all about the mummy factory when he arrived in Alexandria a few days ago, but now he'd learned a lot more than he had come for.

The old man wiped the tear from his cheek and put more sticks on the fire. When the flames came up, he walked back and stood by the bench and spoke again.

"But all the clergy weren't corrupt, my friend. There were still honest priests who conducted funeral services and worked as the embalmers, mummifying the people, and there were some known as hour priests who were astronomers. They kept the calendar and determined lucky and unlucky days, interpreted omens and dreams, and there were others who were doctors of medicine, and some who did magic. Theirs were all honorable and necessary jobs."

He went on talking until it was almost dawn, and when the fire died, they both fell asleep. Hebony woke up before the old man. He didn't want to trouble him anymore, so he carefully opened the old wooden door, just enough for him to slip out, and closed it again, being very careful so its rusty hinges wouldn't squeak out loud and wake up his host.

As he walked through the thicket and toward the road, he wished he could have stayed another day and asked the man more about the cat mummy factory, but he didn't know how he could have done that. He knew that people didn't have the ability to carry on a two-way conversation with a cat. It wouldn't have mattered what question he meowed to him. The old man wouldn't have been able to understand what he asked. To the old man, his words would just have been another cat meow.

That was a pity, Hebony thought to himself, but trying to communicate with a person would have been a waste of his time. But he had been able to understand every word the man had said to him and now had a lot more information to go home with. When he reached the road, he turned right and walked toward the mummy factory. It was the same old bumpy road he'd traveled under the seat of a wagon filled with the bodies of mummified kittens. But this time, he was free and unconstrained. So he jumped over the bumps, took time to smell the flowers and made time to take swats at the little critters that darted around in warm shallow puddles left by a midnight shower the night before. But his hopes of snagging one with his claws were dashed when they all quickly darted away and scurried beneath the rocks and pebbles and hid out of sight. Now his heart was beginning to fill with a feeling of euphoria, and the sound of his purring filled the air. He was happy. He had completed his mission. He'd learned the truth, and he was convinced that his findings would put a stop to the killings. He arrived at the perimeter of the mummy factory around noon and hid under some rocks by the side of the road. He groomed himself, then took cat naps and rested until evening. Then, under the cover of darkness, he crept past the factory and climbed to the top of the hill to spend the night. The next morning, he woke up and walked down the hill toward home.

# CHAPTER 40

# Hebony Goes Home

Home is where the heart is.

As he walked over the grassy lawn that surrounded the house where he lived, he thought about what he was going to say when he arrived. Although he had only been gone but a few weeks, to him, it seemed like a lifetime. Maybe he hadn't found out all there was to know about the mystery of the mummified kittens, but he had learned a lot more than he had been sent for.

He knew a lot about his country, about the priests and priestesses, about cities and temples, fishing boats, a lighthouse, and he'd found his first love. But all he could tell his mother and Annipe was that the priests and common people were raising kittens that were killed, made into cat mummies, and were given to merchants, who sold them to the people who used them as gifts for the gods. He had seen all of that himself, and what he'd learned had been verified by the stories told by the man he'd met just the night before. When he was halfway across the lawn, he looked up at his bedroom window and thought about what he was going to say to his family when he was united with them again.

The first person he saw was his sister Khari. She was sunning in the garden. As he came closer, she was surprised to see him and ran to him, and in a catlike fashion, they rubbed noses and walked around each other, chirping and rattling their teeth. It was the way they had always met. They talked for a short time and then went inside.

"Mom's sleeping," Khari said. "She's going to have kittens soon, you know. She sleeps a lot these days. I'll go and wake her. She will be so glad to see you."

Then his brothers Aten and Kamuzu entered the room. They each said hi, shook paws, and said they would like to hear all about his trip. He quickly covered some of the highlights, but when he came to the part about him being frightened near the mummy factory by what might have been a spy, Aten walked away. This upset Hebony. He wanted to follow Aten and ask him if anything was wrong, but he was interrupted then when his mother came into the room and ran to give him a gentle bump with her head, purred, and then sat next to him.

Everyone but Aten was there when he told his stories over again. When they were finished, he and his mother went to the little room that overlooked the hill, the one he had climbed to find the mummy factory. They talked until they watched the sunset and saw the stars appear. Later that evening, they shared some warm milk and ate the breast of the large rat Aten had killed for the occasion, but Aten didn't join them. When his mother, sister, and Kamuzu left the room, Hebony went and found his brother. He asked Aten what was wrong. He just said he didn't want to talk about it and walked away.

Hebony gave up asking him any more and went to his mother's room and sat by her bedside. She told him how proud she was of him and how glad she was the trip had been successful and so happy that he was still alive. Then Hebony asked her if she knew why Aten was being so cold toward him. She stood up and walked around the room.

"Hebony," she said, "Aten wanted to go with you. He really loves and cares about you. I tried to make him understand that it wasn't possible. I said it wouldn't be safe for two to go, but he wouldn't listen. When you left that morning, he followed you. A few days later, he returned and said you were safe the last time he'd seen you, and then he said he didn't want to talk about it anymore. We haven't discussed it since. Maybe you can talk to him someday. I hate to see my sons not being good friends. Please tell me you will try. Let's go to bed. You must be tired. Oh, and he brought your hat home. He said he found it on a tree branch."

Then Hebony said, "I left it there for a bird to nest in. Remember, you told me never to leave any litter on the trail and to carry out whatever I brought in and to bury what I couldn't carry out. I didn't want to leave anything but my paw prints behind. I thought a bird might use it."

Then his mother said, "I'm glad you did that." And then they both went to bed.

But Hebony didn't sleep well. He was upset about his brother walking away from him when he was telling the story about his trip. He and Aten had been close friends. It just didn't make sense to Hebony. They ran side by side when he was training for the trip. Aten taught him to hide and climb trees. He had been his best coach. Hebony made up his mind. "I have to talk with him," he said to himself, and then he went to sleep.

The next morning, Hebony and his mother went to pray to Annipe and to thank her for watching over him. They told her how grateful they were for what she had done to help their cause and thanked her again. Annipe said she was interested in more details of his trip, so Hebony told her all he had learned. She thanked him for his service and said she would speak with the other gods and the people to see what could be done to end the senseless killing. Then she told Hebony he would be honored with a big festival sometime in the future, but Hebony told her that he didn't want anything to do with festivals.

Hebony didn't find time to talk with Aten again because other problems came up.

# CHAPTER 41

# But Hebony Had a Loose Tongue

Watch what you say. Others may be listening.

It seems that the priests who were behind the killing of kittens were mad at Hebony because they thought he may be the one that had exposed them, and they labeled him the most likely suspect and the whistleblower because he had been away from home and had just returned. The priests had been making a lot of money from the mummies, and they picked Hebony because someone had told them there was a black golden-eyed cat poking around the window at the mummy factory a few weeks ago. Hebony fit the description, so the hunt for him was on.

But Hebony didn't know he was being hunted. He was young and very proud of what he'd done, and he didn't remember what Grosso told him. He went around town and bragged about what he'd done to all his friends, and one of them, for a small bowl of camel's milk, betrayed him. When he didn't come home one night, his mother went in search of him and found him sleeping under a wooden box in an alley off lower Khufu Street. It seems he had been celebrating with some of his buddies again, and he'd fallen asleep in the box after they left. She woke him up and warned him of the great danger he was in and told him that he must go deep into the forest and hide among the wild cats.

So Hebony went into the forest and told the wild cats what he had done, and they offered to help him avoid being captured. There were many furious battles between the wild cats and the men who hunted Hebony, and many a man was scratched, bitten, or mauled by their teeth and claws.

Some were so badly wounded that they gave up the hunt. In other bloody battles, wild cats were wounded, and some died from their injuries. Pet cats came from the surrounding towns to help Hebony, but they didn't know how to fight a battle and didn't want to learn about war. They said they were pacifist, but they were willing to do anything else that would help him stay free.

So Hebony, who knew how to survive, hid in the forest for a long time. The cat people, the cats from town, and all the forest cats worked together to keep him safe and alive. They brought him food when they thought he needed it. Hebony was a cat. He could have lived off the land by using his own cat skills. There was lots of game in the woods. Mice and other things like jerboas were everywhere. There was plenty of water when it rained, but his friends kept in touch with him anyway, and he enjoyed their company. During dry spells, when there wasn't any rain, they brought him camel milk and things to play with. And sometimes, they brought him a little catnip to make him happy.

The plan worked for a long time, and even though the priests surrounded the forest and sent armies of soldiers and armed chariots to patrol the roads that crisscrossed the terrain, Hebony outsmarted them all and survived in the forest using the skills his mother taught him. He learned to live like a forest animal, and he checked their every move like a chess player, even though he'd never played the game.

Then a crazed wild cat named Rudolph betrayed Hebony and told the priests that he was living deep in the center of the forest, where few had ever gone before, and they said that the people were bringing him supplies. Then the priests used their power and made it unlawful for anyone to enter the forest and take supplies to him. Now if anyone were caught supplying Hebony, they would be committing a crime themselves, and if caught, they would be sentenced to years of hard labor in a prison labor camp, and they would be put to death if they were caught a second time. A few people were caught and just given a warning, but that and the possibility of being put to death was more than enough to scare off the rest. Soon nobody dared to go into the woods for fear they might be even suspected of helping Hebony.

Hebony got along without being supplied from the outside, but he grew weaker as time went by.

There were days when it didn't rain, and he had no water to drink. He'd eaten most of the game within the area he felt safe to live in, and he didn't dare leave it. When he heard people hunting for him, he was able to outwit them. The training he had before the trip taught him to hide so well that sometimes a man would almost step on him as he safely hid in one of the many shallow burrows he'd dug near the forest roads and foot trails. Then he got sick and contracted a bad case of roundworm disease, from some uncooked rats he'd eaten, and the cysts from the parasitic worms lodged in his muscles caused him great pain. One day, he had enough. He couldn't go on any longer. He had to eat some decent food.

So under the cover of darkness, he walked into a nearby town and found some leftovers in a trash can behind a small house. A dog inside the house heard him and barked. The owner of the house, a Mr. Kamuze, came out and saw Hebony sitting on the trash can, but Hebony was too weak to run away. Mr. Kamuze picked him up and took him to his tool shed and gave him some food and some rags to sleep on. Of course, at this time Mr. Kamuze had no idea what the cat's name was.

The next morning, Mr. Kamuze took him to his vet for medical attention. The vet's assistant, a Mr. Hasan, helped the vet examine and care for Hebony's sad condition, and when they finished the examination, he offered to take the cat home and continue its care.

But Mr. Hasan thought the cat might be the one that was being hunted by the priests. And after he put Hebony in a cage, he went to lunch and found someone to summon them.

Soon, a chariot arrived at Mr. Hasan's home. Its driver examined the cat and agreed that it must be the one the priests were looking for. It was black, had golden eyes, and was very undernourished. That was enough to satisfy him and put the cat into a cage. The driver thanked Mr. Hasan for being a good citizen and gave him a reward of nine pieces of silver. Then Mr. Hasan gave back one piece of silver to the driver, and one piece each to the two jailers who were riding with him. As they drove away, the driver told the other men that he was almost certain it was the cat the priests wanted and said its name was Hebony. Then he told them not to tell anybody he'd paid them in silver.

He hoped that by sharing the reward with them would keep them from telling anyone what he'd done. He thought that would be the end of it.

Later that week, he lied to the vet by telling him he'd found a good home for the cat. It was something he had done with stray cats many times before. Nobody else, it seems, knew there was a reward for the black cat. It was Mr. Hasan's secret.

# CHAPTER 42

# Hebony Is Taken to Jail

Never resist the arm of the law.

Hebony was taken in paw cuffs to a makeshift jail in the lowest level of a temple. His cell was small, and he had barely enough room to stretch out his tiny body when he wanted to sleep. The only light came through a small window near the top of the jagged rock wall that towered above him. The light that did reach him was dimmed by the dry dust that rose from the old stones that surrounded him.

But it didn't matter. In spite of his golden eyes, there wasn't much to see, and he didn't mind. He needed to sleep, and that would have been hard to do if the cell was bright. But sleeping was hard.

Fleas were biting him, and every time he swung his tail to swat them, more fleas bit him. He had never felt so bad nor been so frightened in his life. He tried to hold his tail still, but it was no use. There were too many fleas. He had to sit on his tail to hold it still so he could take a nap. He'd dealt with fleas before, but nothing like this. Then the jerky bazar movements of a large insect caught his fancy, and Hebony focused his eyes on its antics. It was a scarab beetle pushing a large lump of animal dung across the dirt floor of his cell. Hebony has seen these large insects before, but he'd never had taken the time to study one up close. The lump of dung was about three times the size of the beetle, but it seemed to be pushing with ease as it moved slowly towards a large opening in the stone wall. Upon closer examination, he noticed that the insect was pushing the object with the rear end of its body rather than its head, and he vowed that if he ever got out of his predicament alive, he would ask his mother why it used its head rather than its butt. When the critter finely reached its destination and disappeared into the wall at the tower, Hebony's thoughts returned to his flea infestation.

Scarab beetles were in high esteem in ancient Egyptian mythology. They were a symbol of immortality, resurrection, transformation, and the passage into their afterlife.

It seems that Hebony had been brought to the jail by a chariot sent by some jailers who were hired by some other priests. They were the ones who'd paid Mr. Hasan all the silver. But they had no way to tell the priests at the jail that they were bringing a cat, and they were very surprised when he'd arrived because they didn't know what to do with a cat. In the past, the only thing that had been brought to the jail were people, bad people. This was the first cat, and they were arguing over what they should do with a cat.

And come to think about it, the jailers said it was the first cat they had brought there. That amused him, and he thought to himself, *I guess I am no ordinary cat.* He arched his back up and down again several times. It was the only way he could keep away the pain and stiffness that came from sleeping on the damp floor. When the conversation above him subsided, he looked around the room and noticed a small dish of milk on the floor.

He didn't know where it came from. He walked over and tested it to see if it was fresh. It was, so he drank it. Then there was nothing else he could do, so he laid back down on the floor. He was still so tired from his ordeal. He slept all that day and into the night. But his sleep was plagued with strange dreams that played the same things over and over, and these dreams haunted him long after he woke up.

# Chapter 43

# Hebony's Dreams

Pay attention to your dreams.
Sometimes your dreams are speaking to you.

Of all the dreams he had, two stood out in his mind. One was about a mouse, a mouse who spoke to him. He wasn't surprised by that. He knew mice shared a common language that all animals understood, and they were able to translate each other's words as they were spoken. The mouse said it had come to tell him that the mice weren't upset because cats ate them.

Then the mouse told Hebony that he knew that cats eating mice was something that just fit into the scheme of things. Mice were made to be eaten, and the cats were to eat them. It had always been that way. So now it was a tradition.

But when Hebony was about to thank the mouse for the revelation, another dream invaded his mind before he had the chance.

This was a dream that included a beautiful woman. In the dream, he'd been awakened when a small door opened in a wall of his cell. He recalled looking toward it, arching his back, and letting out a loud hiss in the hope it would scare off whatever or whoever it was. But his aggression was not returned with anger nor another hiss but with kind words from the image of the beautiful woman.

She was about five feet two inches tall, had eyes of blue, a slim build, and a good figure. Hebony was very impressed. But she was dressed differently than any other woman he had seen.

She wore fancy red high-heeled boots up to her knees, a short black miniskirt, and a white blouse with little black bows at the end of each sleeve. There was a ring on every finger, and gold earrings hung from each ear.

Surprised and happy about by what he'd seen in this dream so far, Hebony slowly gained his composure and excused himself for being aggressive. Then he laid down on the floor and rolled over onto his back and started to purr.

The mysterious woman walked over and picked him up and cradled him in her arms. At first, he didn't want to be held by any person he didn't know, and he squirmed to get away. But she held him tightly and began to pet him and spoke to him in a very gentle voice.

"I've been sent to help you, Hebony," she said.

Hebony relaxed and stopped wiggling. At first, he had a little trouble understanding her foreign accent. It wasn't southern, but soon he was able to understand what she was saying. It was something about a trial he would have. He wanted to ask her how she knew his name, but before he could, she spoke again. This time, her voice was a little louder.

"You may have forgotten," she said, "but before you were born, the people who love cats asked the goddess Annipe to have your mother to send one of her kittens on a mission to learn why people were killing little kittens and making them into mummies. She chose you because you were large and brave. You did very well. You solved the mystery, but by doing so, you exposed yourself to the priests that were doing it. That made them mad. They hunted you down, and you hid in the forest until you were so hungry and went into a town. There, the people found you, and now you are in jail and charged with some very serious crimes.

"The people who love cats are proud of you. They don't think you committed a crime, and they're a little sorry that they got you into all this in the first place. But that doesn't matter now. The priests wanted you, and they wanted you dead. I'm sorry it turned out that way. Your people sent me to see if I could help save your life. But you have to help me to do it."

Hebony felt a little smug. He saw himself as a hero, and he was proud of what he'd done.

The strange lady lifted him up and placed him on the floor. Then she looked around his cell and shouted to the rocks that surrounded them.

"Why didn't they give you a bed or even a chair for this room? I'd like to sit down."

Then she leaned back against the rock wall, shook her head, and spoke again in her more gentle voice.

"You should have kept your mouth shut and not bragged about what you'd done. You may have been able to get away with it all. You could have gone back to Alexandria where there were other black cats. Then none of this may have happened. The priests would have still hunted for you, but I doubt if they would have ever found you. They have too many other things on their mind right now. Your crime would have soon been forgotten and become a cold case. It's too bad you went into town and partied that night."

Their time is short. The empire's falling apart.

"Sooner or later, the Romans will take over Egypt, the priests will be out of a job, and someday, the people will no longer be allowed to worship cats. The Romans think cat lovers are members of a pagan cult, and they won't let them worship cats anymore. But I guess you cats will never forget you were once worshipped and treated as gods, and now I expect you would like the people to give you that same level of respect in the future." Hebony replied yes by rapidly nodding his head and, at same time, raising his right paw into the high-four-paw position.

She was really fired up now, and the increase in the volume of her voice scared Hebony.

"But oh no!" she shouted.

"You had to go and tell the world what you'd done. Now you are in jail. In the future, take my advice. Keep your victories to yourself. Real heroes don't brag about what they've done." Hebony smiled and nodded a yes. He'd heard that before from Grosso, and now he wished he'd remembered his advice.

Then as her voice lowered, she said, "Well, what's been done is done. I'm here to help save your life. If the priests find you guilty, and there is little doubt that they will not, you could be put to death. You are being put on trial for being a whistleblower and for treason against the kingdom. If they find you guilty, it gives them the right to kill a cat. They say you broke their law."

She walked around the floor, stopped walking, and spoke again.

"Here are a few things I want you to remember when you go to trial. First of all, keep your mouth shut and don't open it unless you are asked a direct question. Never speak unless you're spoken to."

Hebony didn't understand that. He had always been one to speak his mind, but he said that in this case, he would do his best to keep quiet. Then she waved her boney ring finger in his face.

A finger that seemed to grow longer in his mind as she waved it. Hebony followed the finger with his eyes as if he was being hypnotized.

"I'll be in the courtroom with you, but I may be in a different form than I am now. Let me speak in your place. Don't make a fool of yourself. And groom yourself before you go to court. It might impress the judge."

When she left the cell, Hebony was still dreaming. And in his dream, he saw her pick up the dead mouse, put it into a small bag she carried, and then place a small bowl of something in its place.

Soon after she left, his dream ended, and Hebony woke up. He had slept all that day, and he was groggy from having been asleep so long. When he stood up, he staggered around the cell a little before and he saw a small bowl on the floor of his cell. It was filled with cool camel milk. He wasn't sure where it came from, but then he remembered the mysterious ghostlike woman who had visited him in the dream.

After the mysterious woman's dream ended, Hebony went to sleep again. He was happy when he did, but as soon as he was asleep, a third dream came into his mind. It was a dream about his mother. She seemed to have come out of nowhere, but Hebony recognized her right away, and he was glad to see her. He was missing her, and he was glad to see her again. He'd been thinking about her ever since he left home, and he had a lot of questions that he wanted her to answer. So he stood up and then laid down again and turned up his belly to her. This was done to show his respect to her. She told him to roll over, and when he did, she sat beside him, and he told her that everything had gone well despite of the circumstances. Then she told him that the gods had been keeping her informed of what he'd been doing, and she said that she was proud of him and couldn't wait for him to come home.

# CHAPTER 44

# How Could People Hold
# a Fair Trial for a Cat?

Some things turn out not to be as simple as thought.

How to tri Hebony at his trial was a problem for the priests. They were people, and he was an animal, a cat. To choose a jury of twelve cats would have been the logical choice, but the priests didn't want that. They said it would be too hard for any of them to know what was going on because neither the judge nor any other members of the court would be able to converse with a jury of twelve cats because they couldn't understand what the cats were saying back. However, the cats would understand the words of the people and judge, and they might not follow their orders. Cats don't like to follow orders.

For example, cats come when called, but only if they're in the mood. So at trial, they may not come to the bench when they were called.

It is common knowledge that cats are able to read the minds of people and would know if anyone in the court were trying to trick or mislead them.

Because unlike other animals, cats don't live in flocks, herds, or swarms. They are all individuals. Each cat would think for itself and a jury of cats would never be able to come together to bring a unanimous verdict.

In the end, the priests all agreed that cats would never agree on anything, so they rejected the idea. They wanted a judge and jury that would convict Hebony and a trial where the judge could overrule any of the participants and have complete control over the outcome and the verdict.

Then one of the priests suggested that they might be able to have a trial made up of other animals, like animals everybody understood.

Granted, he said, "No person can carry on a two-way conversation with a camel or a horse, but a domesticated camel can be taught to kneel, to let its rider saddle up, go forward when they said go, and then obey another word that meant kneel down to let them off. Camels learned to obey or be beaten. Beating a cat doesn't work. An abused cat just gets up and walks away. But I think we could make any other animal bend to the ways of the court."

Some of the priests weren't happy about that suggestion, but they all knew there had to be a trial. Hebony had wronged them. He trespassed on their property, gained entrance to their buildings without being invited, and set free the animals they had raised to produce valuable merchandise, like cat mummies, and surely any man educated in the law would agree that he was committing a serious crime, and if convicted, the criminal must be punished."

Most of the priests agreed, but a few of them felt they should consult with all the animal gods before they did it. So they called on all the animal gods of every species and asked each of them for an opinion.

All of them agreed it was a novel idea and said it would be a nice distraction from their daily duties if they were able to do it. Most said they couldn't wait to watch the trial going on from above. With that settled, a simple majority of them approved the idea, and the architects of the trial set out to find the animals they needed.

The animals common in Egypt, at the time, included horses, camels, water buffalos, gazelles, jackass, Nubian ibex, jackals, desert fox, and jerboas, a type of rodent, and domestic dogs. In addition, there were mice and rats that had learned living in cities was better than the desert.

But when they studied the real animals they wanted to enlist and learned their habits, they realized that using real animals was not going to be possible.

Each had different toilet habits. Most of the animals wouldn't be able to sit on the courtroom's only toilet or the chairs.

And some would, no doubt, want to eat one another.

So the priests called back to the gods once again and asked them for even more divine intervention. Then after much discussion, the gods offered them a one-time-only solution.

Their animal trial could be held, but no real animals could be used.

Members of the court would have to wear the headdress of the animal they chose when the court was in session.

It seemed like a crazy idea, but after much discussion and some jokes about who would play the part of the jackass, the vote to do so was more than unanimous because some of them voted twice.

# CHAPTER 45

# Choosing the Dress Code for the Trial

A court is always made up of many odd fellows.

That done a pretrial date was set and soon the people were called and gathered in the courtroom. The judge was the only judge in town, at the time, so he got to choose the people who would serve the court. He said he would assume the part of a camel and would proudly wear the headdress of one in court, because he raised camels on a large tract of land out near the Nubian Waterhole.

The judge asked the clerk of the court to find the men who would serve as jurors and said that he wanted them to come to court wearing the headdress of a jackal. Jackals were common animals who lived throughout the nearby desert, and they were not known to be fair about anything. Jackals sleep most of the day and search for food at night. They never hunted other animals during the daylight, and they'd rather steal the leftovers made from the kills of larger animals. And they were very fond of cat meat and would eat one if they had a chance.

A jury of jackals would surely intimidate the cat.

The courtroom attendants were able to round up fourteen people to dress as jackals, twelve jurors, and two alternates.

When the judge saw the kind of people the clerk had found for the job, he said they'd have to be kept in a cage during the proceedings so they couldn't harm the other people in the courtroom. Then he added, "These are the meanest looking men I have ever seen."

The prosecutor told the judge he wanted to dress as a horse because he kept a lot of cats in his stable to catch the mice.

That didn't make much sense to anyone but the judge, and he said he would allow it.

Two defenders chose the headdress of a desert fox, an animal well known to hunt cats in the desert, but they told the judge that in spite of that, they would do their best to defend Hebony. The judge smiled and accepted him. He had picked them for the role. A third member of the defense team would wear the headdress of a house cat.

The human visitors came from all walks of life, and all wore the head of an animal of their choice. Some were cat lovers. They wore the headdress of a cat, and they sat on the right side of the courtroom. The ones that didn't like cats would wear the head of wild dogs, and they chose to sit on the left side of the courtroom.

The judge had ordered that a wall be built between the rival parties to keep them apart, but it wasn't finished in time, and the trial would have to start without it.

The court attendants, including the clerk of the court and his aides, would all wear the heads of domesticated dogs.

During the trial, all the dogs but the clerk would be allowed to totter around the courtroom and poke their nose up somebody's butt or bury their head in someone's lap after they'd drunk from the courthouse toilet. It was something all dogs seem to enjoy doing.

The jerboas, a wild rodent, were too far away in the back of the room, and field mice watched in through the windows.

Some of the cats that had helped Hebony hide from the priests requested time on the court's ducat as *amicus curiae* or a friend of the court. They wanted to help Hebony's defense team. But they were denied the right to speak in his defense.

# CHAPTER 46

# Hebony Is Taken to the Courtroom

Every cat has its day.

The night before his trial, he was visited by the kind woman in his dream again. She gave him a little more advice about his behavior and a dish of cool camel milk. The milk had been spiked with catnip to calm his nerves and help him sleep. But when he woke up the next morning, his mind was not free of the milk's slumbering effect, and he was feeling a little groggy when three men who wore the headdress of pit bulldogs came into his cell.

They put a tight stud-filled collar around his neck, hooked a leash to it, and led him up a flight of stone steps that led to a room above. He was then taken into an already filled courtroom and told to curl up on a chair with a maroon pillow.

They attached the outer end of his leash to a ring on the floor and left him napping on the chair.

When he woke up, he couldn't believe what he was seeing.

When he looked to his left, there were three people seated alongside him seated in similar chairs but without a pillow. They were not chained to their chairs.

One of them looked like the mysterious lady who had brought him the cool camel milk in his dream. Today she wore the headdress of a cat. He looked at her and gave the best smile a cat could give. She nodded her head and smiled back. Then he knew it must be her.

Next to her sat two people he had never seen before. One had the headdress of a fox and the other that of a Nubian ibex. The ibex had two long black horns that curved far over the back of his chair.

The other man who would have been dressed as an owl had gone hunting rabbits that morning and had forgotten to show up on time. But when the ibex, who was the original alternative, found that he would have to remain in his seat throughout the trial because his horns caught in the back of his chair whenever he stood up was excused. And the man dressed as an owl came into the courtroom, put two dead rabbits under his chair, and although the lady dressed as a cat objected, the judge allowed him to be seated along with the defense and the trial went on.

On the other side of the room across a hallway were three more people seated in three chairs. Two of these men wore the headdress of a horse and the others that of a gazelle.

In front of him, up on the top of a platform, was a long black heavily-carved, wooden table with an empty chair behind it. In front of the platform, down on the courtroom floor, stood an old robed man holding a long stick in his right hand.

Behind the wooden table, on the platform, and to its right was a cage of men headdressed as jackals. They were jumping up and down against the strong reed bars that held them in. As they jumped, they let out sharp barks, and Hebony shuddered with fear. These were the first jackals he had ever seen up close, and he hoped that the bars of the cage would hold them. But he relaxed when some of the people wearing the headdresses of wild dogs shouted for them to be quiet.

Behind him, in a place where he had to squirm around to see, there were people wearing the headdress of house cats. The cat lovers wore green caps, and the people who didn't fully appreciate cats wore red caps. The wives, girlfriends, and friends of members of the court sat behind them and far behind them sat the jerboas. Hebony couldn't see them, but he could smell them, and that made his mouth water.

Hebony had been told that jerboas were good to eat, but that was only if you were able to get past their foul smell.

He didn't notice the mice looking in the windows nor the faces of his few cat friends who had been told to leave after the judge denied them of their right to speak in his defense. They were disappointed by that, but they decided to hang around anyway and watch the proceedings through the windows.

All those cats were hungry that day, but they didn't think it would be right for them to disturb everything by chasing mice around and eating them during the trial, so they made a deal with the mice.

They told the mice that they wouldn't be chased or be eaten if they would repay the favor by doing one for a cat someday. The mice agreed, and all went well.

# Chapter 47

# Hebony Hears the Charges Against Him

There comes a time when you learn why you're there.

During the times Hebony had been in the courtroom before, the court had not been in session, and everyone there was talking. He had been surprised and amused by the sight of everyone wearing an animal headdress. His mysterious lady friend hadn't explained that to him, and he wondered if all the people at a trial always dressed that way. He hoped he could learn the answer, and he was thinking about who he could ask. Then the room went silent, and everyone went to their place and he stood up on his chair, and he followed suit as he watched a camel-headed man walked into the room, climbed the steps of the platform, and sat in the chair behind the bench. This man wore a long black robe.

Soon a person dressed as a dog stood in front of the bench pounded his stick on the courtroom floor and cried out, "Order in the court. The Honorable Judge, Mr. For-a-Camel, is presiding. All ye stand up. This court is now in session."

Everyone remained standing. Hebony followed suit by standing on four feet. Then the camel-head-dressed judge hammered his gavel on the table and said, "You may be seated."

And everyone sat down but the clerk of the court, who remained standing, and then he pounded his long stick on the floor and spoke out in a deep bass voice, saying, "Hear ye, hear ye, hear ye. The circuit court of the City of Alexandria is now in session."

Then the judge, whose full name was Id.walk.a.mile For.a.camel, pounded his gavel on the bench and repeated that his court was in session, and he asked the clerk to read the charges Hebony was charged with. The clerk remained standing as he spoke.

"This court has been convened to determine the guilt or innocence of an animal, a cat, known as Hebony, son of Annipe, a female street cat from the Hither Lands. All Ye have mercy upon his kha." The latter meant his soul.

Then the old clerk, who had still not sat down since he'd come into the room, read the charges from a long-ornamented papyrus scroll. His voice trembled, and his whole body shook as he read, "The accused, Hebony of the Hither Lands, is charged with the following crimes: (1) Entering without breaking into a building known only as Building Number Seven, (2) the release of live property housed within that building, kittens who are said to have been born and reared with the permission of their owners, to be sold as pets to people in the homes of wealthy subjects and the pharaohs, (3) exposing the true nature of that complex, which shall not be disclosed at this trial, (4) the crime of whistleblowing, and (5) the most heinous and serious crime of them all is that of treason against his country. Each of these five charges are high crimes and misdemeanors against the state, and in this case, are all considered to be crimes of high treason."

Then he spoke in a voice that was little more than a whisper, "Should this black cat be found guilty of one or more of these crimes, he will be sentenced to death, and may the gods have pity upon him."

# CHAPTER 48

# The Court Is Now in Session

The day of judgment begins early in the morning.

Now that the court was formally opened and all the other introductory speeches were over, the clerk of the court was called to speak to the members of the court and the people assembled there, and he spoke in his formal manner.

"Be ye all aware this court is still in session. No one is allowed to speak from now on unless he or she is called upon by the judge. Hear ye, hear ye, hear ye."

The judge didn't need the clerk to repeat all the "hear yeas," but hearing them made him feel more important.

When everyone was seated, the judge asked the members of the prosecution and the defense to stand up, raise their right hand, and say they would tell the truth, only the truth, and not lie or disobey the rules of his court. When they were seated, the judge, being careful not to disturb his camel headdress, ran his right hand through his gray hair and pointed to the defense table where the man who he appointed to be Hebony's court-appointed defense attorney sat.

The man, who was now wearing his headdress of a fox, stood up and walked slowly around the room, pointing his finger at Hebony and shaking his head from side to side without saying a word. Then he turned and spoke to the bench.

"Your Honor, I am here to defend the accused. I am an unbiased person who loves both cats and dogs. Being a fox today will have no bearing on my actions. My client tells me that he pleads not guilty, and he puts himself at the mercy of the court. He feels he did something that needed to be done. He said it was not right that priests should be allowed to kill cats when it is still a very serious crime for all people. My client says no person should be above the law. He also tells me he cannot understand the language of the other animals in the room and asks that you delay his trial until the court provides him with a translator. Hebony is only five months old, and I ask the court to honor his request."

With that, the prosecutor, a horse-headed man, stood up.

"I object!" he cried.

The judge sustained the objection, and the prosecution spoke on.

"It is well known that all animals, except the people, understand the language of all the other animals. The defense is well aware of that fact, and he is using this tactic only to delay the trial. We people are the only animal the gods failed to bestow the ability of universal speech. Cats don't admit it, but they can understand every word spoken, no matter what animal speaks it. That includes the people. If one of us calls our cat to come for treats, the cat comes running. It understands the word treats. If you tell your wife to make an appointment to take the cat to the vet, the cat hides under the bed. Your Honor, even without speaking, that cat can read your mind when it comes to that subject.

"No cat needs a translator. They are born with a translator in their head. If a horse sees a cat in its way, the horse whinnies words that warn the cat. The cat understands the horse, and it moves out of its way. People don't move out of the way of a horse until they see the horse coming."

Hebony laughed out loud when he heard the arguments of rebuttal, and the judge pointed at him and said, "One more outburst from you, Mr. Cat, and you will be removed from my courtroom."

A smile came to Hebony's face, and he raised his paw to cover it. Seeing his smile had gone unnoticed by the judge, he attempted to speak again. But before he could get a word out, the fox-headed man spoke again, even though the prosecution had objected.

"My client has never seen a horse. I object to his objection. How does the prosecution know what this cat would do in a case like that? His objection is irrelative. I ask that the court instruct the prosecution to end this line of questioning."

The judge shook his fist and banged his gavel, but the prosecutor jumped out of his seat, pointed his finger at the fox-headed man, and cried out in a loud voice, "I object, I object! I even inject! Or whatever." And the prosecutor went on with his objection.

"The defense insults my integrity. He is well aware that cats have unbelievable language skills. It's obvious that it is the wish of the defense to end this trial as soon as possible so his client can return home to his family. We have come here today to learn the truth. I believe this cat has committed many serious crimes, and I plan to present evidence that will prove his guilt beyond the shadow of a doubt."

The fox-headed man jumped up from his seat, disregarded a warning from the judge, and said, "I object to the objection."

But by this time, nobody remembered what the objection was about or who had made it in the first place, but the fox-headed person spoke on without missing a syllable.

"Hebony was too young to understand the gravity of the mission he was sent upon. He was obeying his mother who told him that the gods asked her to send him. He only went to please her and the gods. I demand a delay. My client has never seen a horse before, let alone an owl or a gazelle. None of these animals are native to the part of the country where he was born. Members of the court, we have here a young cat, not yet mature. He knows little of the working of a court. How can we expect him to understand what is going on here? He has the mind of a three-year-old child. I beg the court to delay this trial and reconsider. I object to the objection."

The judge, not knowing how to resolve two objections, nodded and banged his gavel four times.

Hebony couldn't help himself, and he broke out into another fit of laughter, and everyone in the courtroom turned to look at him.

He was rolling over on his seat. He had been able to understand every word that was said by both of them. He'd never seen the man who was defending him before, but now he knew they were going to get along well together.

The judge banged his gavel on the bench again, brought his left hand up to his face, and brought it down palm-first toward the cat and said "Sit," as if Hebony were his dog. But it didn't do anything to Hebony because he was already sitting.

Then the judge nodded his head and said, "The objection is sustained. The prosecution may continue his discourse, but he must rephrase his line of questioning and keep his words within the limit and width of his discourse. I order both of you to stay in your seats. I will no longer tolerate your kind of behavior in my courtroom. You are both acting like jackals."

Neither of them wasn't quite sure if they were sure what the judge meant by limits and width, so they went back to sit in their respective seats.

Then the judge pointed at Hebony and said, "If there are any more outbreaks of laughter, Mr. Cat, you will be sent to your cell, and your trial will go on without you. I have warned you for the last time."

Hebony wanted to speak, but he held back his words when he saw the cat-headed woman seated next to the fox-headed man nod her head toward him. Hebony wisely interpreted the nod to mean he should not speak. He looked down at the floor and didn't say another word.

# CHAPTER 49

# The Trial Goes On

It isn't over until it's over.

With the interruptions over, the court resumed with the proceedings. But before the judge could say a word, the horse-headed man and his partner, a gazelle-headed man, pushed their chairs back, stood up, and appeared to be approaching the bench. But instead, they walked over and stood in front of the defense table.

The horse-headed man turned and pounded his fist on his desk, pointed at the fox-headed man, and said in a loud voice, "What does a fox know about cats? I've had to sleep with our cat after I had an argument with my wife. I know cats very well. They are a lot smarter as a tiny little kitten than an adult fox. There is an old fable that will substantiate that.

"Once upon a time and a long time ago, an old crow made a fool of a fox when the fox couldn't drink water from a pitcher because the water was deep at the very bottom, and the pitcher was too heavy to be pushed over. So the thirsty fox watched as the crow flew up and down, dropping pebbles into the pitcher until the water reached the top. Then the crow drank the water at its lip. When the fox tried to climb to the top of the pitcher to reach its lip, the pitcher fell over, and the fox went away thirsty. You see, even birds have more brains than a fox. I request you ask this fox-headed idiot to leave this courtroom."

The judge pounded his gavel on the bench again, but this time, the sounds were muffled by the barks of the jackals who were awakened by all the noise. The judge pounded his gavel again and again and ordered the clerk to silence the members of the jury.

When that ended the barking, the judge ordered the horse-headed man and his partner, a gazelle-headed man, to return to their seats. They reluctantly obeyed the judge, but the horse-headed man whinnied out loud as he went to his seat, and this brought much laughter from the cat people in the back rows, and it amused Hebony.

Then the cat-headed woman stood up and asked to address the bench. She spoke in a high-pitched catlike voice.

"I know this court is in session, but I beg you to allow a short recess so I may speak to my client in private. The poor little fellow looks like he's stressed out, and I would like a little time alone with him to explain what's going on. May we have the use of the jury room?"

The judge granted her a short recess and stood up and went to his chambers to use his private bathroom. When the recess was over, the cat-headed woman brought Hebony back to the courtroom and chained him to his chair. Then the recess went on until all the other people returned from the one and only public bathroom there was in the courthouse. When everyone was seated, the trial resumed.

The judge thumped the gavel once and asked the clerk of the court to refer to him from now on as just the judge, and he asked that everyone else to stop using their silly animal names, like fox-headed man and cat-headed woman. He said these names were too hard for him to keep track of, and it was more than likely the same for the members of the jury or for anyone who may attempt to read the transcript.

That said, the judge turned around in his chair and banged his gavel on the jackals' cage several times to see if they were awake and paying attention. They were not. They were sleeping and not paying any attention, but that didn't matter to the judge, and he said to himself, "Mmmmm, I'll let sleeping dogs lie."

Then the judge ordered the members of the defense and prosecution to approach the bench. Then Mr. Ammons, for the defense, previously known as the fox-headed man, and Kitty the cat head-dressed spinster, approached. As did two members of the prosecution, who both had worn the headdress of a horse, a Mr. Amasis and Mr. Menna walked up to the bench together, frowning at the other. When they reached the bench, the judge asked them if they would be willing to arbitrate some of their differences with each other so the trial could continue without any more interruptions. They both told him they had settled them during the recess and promised to be more civil to everyone in the future.

Then the judge asked all the members of prosecution and the defense teams to step closer to the bench, then he cupped his hand over his mouth so the people in the room wouldn't be able to read his lips and see what he was saying, and he said to them in a little more than a whisper, "I have a wrestling match this afternoon, and I would like to be there on time. Can we get this silly trial over quickly so I can meet with my opponent on time? I'd like to end this trial so we can all go home early. I'm going to find a way to charge this cat guilty no matter what any of you have to say. My mind has been made up."

The judge, sure that no one else had heard his whisper, excused them, and they went back to their seats. What the judge didn't know was that the clerk of the court had heard every word he said, and the scribe had written it into the record. They wanted to have some dirt on the judge just in case they needed a favor from him in the future.

When Mr. Ammons and Kitty were seated, they took a little time to arrange all the items on their desk. Then Kitty leaned over to Mr. Ammons and said, "I'm not about to let that cat be taken away from this room unless he gets a fair trial. I want the jury, as bad as it looks, to decide his guilt or innocence, not just some old crooked judge who must have his hands in the pockets of the priests."

The prosecution shuffled their papyrus documents on their table too and then asked permission to address the court. The judge granted permission, and Mr. Menna stood up.

"I don't think this court can ever reach a fair verdict. The mixture of animals assembled here are not wise enough to understand the workings of the court."

There was a rumbling in the courtroom as all the other animals objected.

"We feel that more educated animals, like camels, should judge this cat. Any animal that can cross the desert without a drink and find its way home has to be more worthy of making a decision than any horse. Horses get lost unless there is a barn to return to. We admit we are both horses, but we would decline any request to find more horses to try this cat. Some say we should let polecats or foxes decide Hebony's fate. A fox can only find its way home if its nose is to the ground, and nobody would want to be in a room full of polecats. And we have already concluded that cats shouldn't try Hebony either. We don't trust them. They're a biased bunch. A clowder of cats would release the accused on merit alone, and justice would not be served."

The judge knew the prosecution was trying to butter him up, but he didn't say or do anything to stop it.

That said, the woman, who we know now as Kitty, got up out of her seat and walked over to the prosecutor's desk. She accused Mr. Akhem of degrading cats and told him that his big fancy words, like clowder of cats, didn't intimidate her and said she could use big words too.

She said he was hippophobic and maybe a misanthrope at the same time. Then she took off one of the red spiked-heeled boots off and hit him on the head with it. The whole courtroom was so stimulated by her action that laughter, followed by mayhem, broke out.

The judge pounded his gavel on the bench to call for order, but it did no good. The court was totally out of order. Hebony started laughing again, and this time, he fell out of his chair.

The people who had different opinions about cats and had been seated on either side of the courtroom started making nasty catcalls at each other and threw their shoes across the aisles. The jerboas, who were ailurophobes, started to squeak and jump up and down. The jackals, who normally sleep during the day, were not paying attention to the proceedings. They woke up, broke out of their cage, and ran all over the courtroom.

The people ran out the only door. The jackals, who couldn't find the door, jumped out the windows and headed back home to their wives and girlfriends as the mice at the windows ran to their holes and the cats chased them, just for the fun of it. Then all was quiet, except for peeping sounds that came from six baby birds in a bird's nest high up under the eaves of the courthouse. The baby birds were hungry and were crying because the chaos in the courthouse had scared their parents away, and they hadn't returned with any bugs to feed them.

# CHAPTER 50

# The End Looked Near but Was Not

It isn't over until it's over.

When the commotion ended inside the courtroom and the judge was able to gain his composure, he found his gavel among the debris and pounded it hard on the bench as he said, "I should call a mistrial. My jury has run away. The behavior of the members of this court and those in attendance have tested my patience and have ruined my day. I would call a mistrial if there wasn't so much time left in this day."

Then he reassembled his courtroom, pounded his gavel three times, ordered twelve people from the audience to stand up and be sworn in as jurors by the clerk, and said he would continue the proceedings until sundown, and if they weren't finished by then, court would convene again early tomorrow morning when the shadow of the hand of the sundial covers the image of the ox."

When all was said and done and the room was peaceful again, the judge told everyone to remain in their seats and asked the clerk to strike the floor with his staff. The clerk did so, and after a loud thump, he said, "The court is back in session. The proceedings may resume."

The judge hit the bench with his gavel again to make sure everyone was awake and then asked Mr. Akhem and Kitty to come to the bench.

"Mr. Akhem," he said, "your behavior in my court has been deplorable. I should have you disbarred. And as for you, Miss Kitty, whatever your qualification may be, I am ashamed of you too. If you ever appear in my court again, I hope you will have learned your manners and will keep your shoes on your feet."

Then the judge dismissed them both with orders to behave themselves, and they returned to their seats.

When everyone was seated, the judge asked if there were any witnesses who wished to speak, and the clerk said yes and then said, "The prosecution asks that we call Mr. Kamuze."

Mr. Kamuze was the person said to have captured Hebony in the trash can behind his home.

When Mr. Kamuze arrived at the bench, he was asked to raise his hand and say he would tell the truth. Then Mr. Akhem asked him, "Are you the person that captured the cat known as Hebony?

"Yes" was the reply. "He came into my yard during the dark of night in hopes, I guess, of finding some food."

"How did you come to that conclusion?" Mr. Akhem asked.

"Because he was inside my trash can, and he looked very thin."

"Then you fed him and gave him a bed in your tool shed, is that correct?" Mr. Akhem asked.

"Yes," Mr. Kamuze replied.

"And first thing in the morning, I took him to a Hippiatroi, the horse doctor, because it was my day off. I asked his assistant, Mr. Hasan, to examine the cat. He did, and later that day, he told me that although the cat was weak, he thought he'd be okay once he started eating again. He said he might suffer from ringworm, but there wasn't much he could do about that. I didn't want a cat for a pet, so I told Mr. Hasan to see what he could do with him. I don't think he knew that the cat was wanted for some crime he'd committed.

"If he had, he would have brought it up, and that would have interested me. I thought a cat would never be a criminal. I thought they were honest little critters. My dog is always stealing food off my table. You can never trust a dog. Mine even takes my shoes, and…"

Mr. Akhem stopped him in midsentence, and Mr. Kamuze was excused, and then he called on Mr. Hasan, the vet's assistant, who thought the cat might be wanted for a crime, but they didn't call him Hebony at that time.

When Mr. Hasan reached the bench, he raised his hand and was sworn in. "Mr. Hasan," Mr. Akhem asked, "how did you know the cat seated in this courtroom might be the cat now known in this room as Hebony?"

"Because he was black, sir, jet-black, and very thin, and he looked like he hadn't eaten in a long time, and the vet agreed he was malnourished. That means he was very thin, Your Honor, or something like that, and he matched the description of a cat some people were looking for."

Then Mr. Hasan went on.

But before he could speak, Mr. Ammons, for the defense, cried out, "I object. Any number of cats could have black fur."

"No," Mr. Hasan replied. "Black fur is not known in any cats that live where I do, or at least I never heard of one."

"You have never heard of one, you say?" Mr. Ammons replied. "Now that doesn't mean there couldn't be one now, does it?"

Mr. Hasan answered, "Yes, I guess not."

Then Mr. Menna jumped up out of order, looked to the witness, and said, "Do you consider yourself to be an expert on cats, Mr. Hasan?"

Mr. Hasan trembled as he answered.

"No."

Then Mr. Akhem jumped up and shouted to the judge, "The defense is trying to intimidate his own witness again! I object."

The judge sustained the objection and allowed Mr. Menna to go on, and no one objected, so Mr. Menna went on with his questioning.

"Now, Mr. Hasan, if you say you are not an expert on cats, but you must admit that you have not seen a large number of cats during your lifetime. Is that true?"

Mr. Hasan said he had only seen the ones that were brought into the vet's office, and he added that the vet saw more dogs than cats. Then he said that someone told him that people in robes were looking for a cat that looked like the one you're calling Hebony. It was a black cat with golden eyes, like that one, pointing to Hebony. Then Mr. Hasan spoke aloud, "That's why I grabbed him after the vet was through with him, and later I knew he was wanted for a crime, and I called the priests to come get him. They were the ones that wanted him."

"Is it true that you were paid several pieces of gold in reward for his capture?" Mr. Menna asked.

"Yes," he replied. "Nine pieces, sir, but they were silver, not gold, and I gave one to each of…" Then he mumbled something more about him not wanting to incriminate himself and put the jailers in danger.

Mr. Menna knew that no one else heard what Mr. Hasan mumbled either, so he let him mumble on. The word yes was enough for him, and he paused and spoke to the witness again.

"Now might I correctly assume then that you may have been more interested in the reward than you were of being certain that the cat you turned over to the priests was the right cat?"

Mr. Ammons interrupted and objected again. The judge sustained the objection, but then Mr. Menna dropped his line of questioning and said to the judge, "I don't think it's right to keep badgering this witness. It is obvious he is not an expert on cats. He thought the vet was harboring a dangerous fugitive. Any decent person would have done the same. But at the same time, Mr. Hasan's testimony leads us to assume that he may have identified the wrong cat. If that were correct, the cat we have in this courtroom may not be the cat who committed the crime, and the guilty cat may still be living. If that were the case, it would be free to be sent again to do more exploration into the activities of the priests."

The judge dismissed Mr. Hasan and thanked him for his testimony and for his service to the court. Then the judge asked the clerk of the court if there were any witnesses who had been called by the court but had not as yet appeared. The clerk said there was one cat who said he'd seen Hebony near Building Number Seven at the cat mummy factory one night.

With that, Mr. Menna asked the judge to delay the trial until the mysterious witness could be found and brought to testify. He said he thought he might be able to help clarify things for the prosecution. Mr. Ammons stood up, agreed, and said would like that person to testify too so he could cross-examine him. But that person could not be found.

Then the clerk told the judge that he had been told that there was a strange cat seen hanging around the mummy factory on a night in question. They found that cat, but it failed to answer the subpoena it was served. Now it was nowhere to be found. The judge said he was sorry that the cat didn't come because he would have been very amused by another cat coming to his court, especially if they were to get into a fight.

Then with no more witnesses to call, the judge said he didn't think there was enough evidence for the new jury to convict Hebony or to find him not guilty, and he said he didn't trust his new jury to come to the verdict he wanted anyway. So he called for a mistrial amid objections from both the defense and prosecution.

# CHAPTER 51

# Another Surprise

Sometimes a friend in need, finds a friend indeed.

But when the judge stood up and was about to order the clerk to clear the courtroom, there was a loud tapping on one of the windows at the rear of the room and all the people, Hebony, and all of the lawyers included, turned in their seats to see who was tapping. The judge heard it too, but he wasn't a bit happy about it. He had a meeting to go to, but about all he could do was sit back down, bang his gavel down on the bench, and call for order.

The tapping was coming from the claws of a large orange cat. Hebony was the only one who knew who the cat was, but he was wise enough to keep his mouth shut.

It was Grosso, the cat Hebony had met at the chariot race. If Hebony hadn't been chained to his chair, he might have got up and run to greet Grosso, but something told him to sit tight.

It seems the judge thought that Grosso could have been one of the cats that had failed to appear at court after they'd been served with a subpoena, and if he was one of them, he thought he might be able to enjoy seeing two cats wrestle in his courtroom after all.

With that in mind, he asked the clerk to invite the cat in. The old clerk stumbled to the rear window and opened it, and Grosso jumped in.

He thanked the clerk, and then with a meow, he weaved between his legs as the two of them walked toward the bench. He didn't take time to say hi to Hebony, but right then, it wasn't part of his plan. When the clerk and Grosso reached the bench, the clerk sat down, and Grosso stood up on his two hind feet, looking up at the judge.

The judge was about to ask the clerk to unchain Hebony so the games could begin, but before he opened his mouth to speak, Grosso bowed and started talking to the judge.

He was aware the judge wouldn't be able to understand a word he said to him, so long before he came up to the window to tap his way into the courtroom, he'd asked the gods to interpret whatever he said and to put his words into the mind of the judge.

This was done the same way your cat tells you something it wants you to know. They do it with a combination of meows, burps, pantomime, and gestures, which what they were thinking about. Like "I want to go outside, or my litter box is dirty." But with the help of the gods, this cat could send Grosso's words into the mind of the judge, so from then on, whenever Grosso spoke, everything he said was planted in the mind of the judge, who now, surprised as he was, sat bewildered as he listened to his mind.

"Mr. Judge," Grosso said, "you didn't know this, but after you denied all the cats that came to testify in Hebony's defense and ordered us not to speak with the accused, we went out behind the courtroom, and we've been watching your proceedings through those windows."

He pointed to the back of the courtroom.

"When I was younger, Your Honor, I was a courthouse cat. My job was to keep the courtroom free of mice, and I was good at it. There never was a mouse that ran up some old lady's leg or up and under the judge's robe. But on the brighter side, while I was working there, I learned a lot about courtroom procedure, and I want to tell you that I think you are a poor excuse for a judge. I'm also well aware that you thought I was going to wrestle that cat over there." He pointed to Hebony. "I know a lot about you because your whispers the other day traveled all the way to the back of the room and beyond. Cats have supernatural listening abilities."

"When I first came up to the bench, you thought you wouldn't be able to understand anything I said, but now you're listening with your mind. I took care of that. Is it working?"

The judge nodded his head, and Grosso spoke on. "Cats have the power to send their thoughts to all other animals without an interpreter, but in your case, I had to get help from the gods. They will understand what I say and then pass it on to you. I think you understand me now."

The judge nodded again, and Grosso spoke on. "Now I didn't ask the gods to share this gift to anyone else in this room. I didn't wish to harm your reputation with the lawyers and the people. They'll just sit back and wonder why I gesture and talk without emitting any sound. This is mind control, Mr. Judge. It's ESP. All cats have it. They may have invented it.

"Now I'd like to tell you that based on my limited knowledge of the law, that circus you've had going on here for the past few days was in no way the way to run a trial. First of all, the cat you call Hebony shouldn't have been brought to court in the first place. The priests had a very weak case. He didn't commit any serious crimes. Maybe the one for trespassing was, but that's not a serious crime in the first place. In most cases, a decent judge would have dismissed the case before a trial began. He may not have seen the 'No trespassing' signs in the dark. This cat was sent on a mission of discovery. At no time during his training was he taught to fight and kill or break the law. Besides, he is just a kitten.

"He was sent to learn if the rumor about kittens being killed was true, as it is strictly against the law for anyone to kill a cat throughout the empire, even if it happens by accident. He went willingly and bravely into the unknown, all alone, to learn the truth. He went where no cat had ever gone before. He found the evidence he was looking for. He returned home with it. He told the cat gods what he found, and they communicated it to the people.

"Then when he discovered that the priests were killing the cats, he was the only one who was targeted, hunted down, arrested, and charged with serious crimes. No priests were charged or arrested, and they were the ones killing cats when it was strictly against the law."

Then Grosso stood up on his hind legs and shouted, "No one should be above the law!" Then he went back down on all fours, paused, and said in a soft voice, "Now, I ask you, sir, what was his crime?" And as he shook his head from side to side, he waited for it to sink in before he began speaking again. "It was said, he let some kittens free from their cages. You never called anyone to the bench who could testify to that. Those kittens may have found their own way out of their cage, and for all we know, the priests may have had Hebony arrested to cover up their own crimes or mistakes. One of them may have forgotten to close the kittens' cage. The woman who fed the kittens every day might be a prime possibility. Did you subpoena her? You don't have to answer my question. I already know the answer."

Grosso had learned to be a talented public speaker when he was a courtroom cat, and he'd learned a lot about the law too.

If cats were politicians, he would have been in line for a very high office.

Then he spoke on.

"You never called for or allowed any witness or witnesses to speak of anything in my friend's defense. You just sat back and allowed your lawyers to argue with one another over mundane matters, such as why a crow was smarter than a fox. And you never allowed the accused to speak in his own defense. There were no gods called except the ones you called to ask if it was okay to use animals or people with an animal headdress to take part of your trial. You never asked anyone to testify that the gods had any role in his case. I heard the gods told the people to send Hebony because the people were afraid to go themselves. You might have asked some of those people to testify.

"The only witness you did call was the poor vet's assistant, and he had nothing to do with the accused's innocence or guilt. And when he testified, you sat back and watched as the prosecutors and defense attorneys badgered poor Mr. Hasan like a bunch of cats playing with a mouse. And now, you've become tired of being the judge. You want to get to your wrestling match on time, so now you may want to call for a mistrial. That's a cop out, Mr. Judge."

The judge had understood every word Grosso said, but he didn't care. He was in a big hurry to get to that wrestling match, so he ordered the clerk to escort Grosso out the door and tell him that if he was seen in Alexandria again, he would be arrested and sent to jail.

So fearing for his own welfare, Grosso went home and waited, until his friends told him what happened to Hebony at his new trial with a new judge.

The first trial, which wasn't quite fair to begin with, was over, and Hebony was taken back to his cell to await a retrial.

Later that night, as Hebony tried to sleep, he wondered if his brother Aten could have been one of the missing cats that didn't appear in court. And he wondered, if it had been Aten, would he have testified that it was him at the mummy factory and helped to convict him, or would he have told the court "I was never sure who it was that I saw?"

# CHAPTER 52

# A Kangaroo Trial in a Land Without Kangaroos

Some days in court were very long and unfair, and
some were very quick, and very unfair.

A few days later, Hebony was taken from his cell again and brought back up to the same courtroom. The trial with animal-headdressed people was over, and his first judge had turned the trial over to another jurisdiction and to a new judge that was appointed by the priests. Hebony searched the room for the mysterious lady who had worn the cat's headdress, but she was not there. The court had appointed another person to defend him. Now his defense was in the hands of a man who was a good friend of the priests, and he did more to convict Hebony than he did to acquit him.

When all the members of that court had their say, and there wasn't much said, the judge asked Hebony if he had anything to say to his jury of twelve hooded priests wearing red robes. Hebony stood up and told the judge that he had been told not to speak to anybody but the lady who had been at his first trial. The judge told him to sit down, and he didn't allow him to say another word, nor did he ask for any other witnesses in his defense. The jury was asked for a

164

verdict, and they all cried "Guilty." The judge struck the table three times with his gavel, and he repeated, "Guilty as charged." Then Hebony was returned to a lonely cell down deep in another stone tower on the other side of town.

# CHAPTER 53

# Friends from the CGS Make a Plan to Break Hebony Out of Jail

There comes a time when everyone needs
a little help from their friends.

The next morning, Hebony was asleep on the hard stone floor of his cell when he heard something scratching on the outside of his prison wall. He was locked up in another stone tower, and like most stone towers, its stones were not fitted tightly together when it was built, and there were tiny little cracks and small openings between the rocks. He got up from the floor, stretched his stiff body, and walked slowly to the place where he'd first heard the sounds. Then he found that if he tipped his head just right, he could see out into the courtyard, and when he got it just right, he saw several cats lounging nearby. When he scratched on his side of the wall and meowed a few times, a large male tabby cat came his way and spoke to him.

He told Hebony that his name was Tom Dooly and said he was a friend of Khari's.

Hebony felt a lump well up in his throat when he heard the name Khari. She was the cat he had met long ago on a park bench in Alexandria. He thought he would never hear of her again.

"Yes, I…I…I remember a Khari," Hebony said. "Is she a white cat that lives under the house that has flowers all around it? If your answer is yes, that's her. I do…I do know her."

The tabby cat replied, "Yes, that's the one. She was aware that a big trial was going on in Alexandria, but she didn't know it was your trial until she heard your name mentioned. She has a job now. She is the editor in chief of the CGS, the Cat Gossip Service. It's a word-of-mouth verbal service cats use to keep up with the latest news. She wants me to tell you that she thinks you got a rotten deal. She said you never told her what your mission was about, but now she is very proud of you for what you did. We're going to find a way to get you out of there and save your life."

Hebony's feeling of depression turned to joy as he thought about it. A few minutes ago, he thought he was doomed. Now he had hope. The tabby cat had walked away, but he said they would return and break him free. So Hebony took a much-needed nap, and this time, he slept without any bad dreams.

Hebony was happy about the news, but now he knew that it would have put Khari on the spot. She was the Editor in Chief of the Cat Gossip Service and now was willing to help him, even though he'd walked out on her and never said a word after she had had let him spend the night with her.

But Khari had already put that aside and was still fond of him and not about to let anything happen to him. But first, she would have to find out what was on the minds of the priests before she could make a plan to rescue him. So she asked all the members of her staff to meet her at their headquarters, which was located in the highwater section of Alexandria.

The office was in the basement of an abandoned nightclub on Dierk's Street. In better days, the nightclub had been a meeting place for cat lovers. Cat lovers are just normal people who like cats, but every now and then, they wanted to enjoy a little social interaction with people as well. So when their long day's work was over, they would meet at the nightclub to hear the bands, dance, and drink the finest Egyptian wines. Sometimes, one or more of them would bring a cat to the club to show it off to their friends.

But unbeknownst to then and anyone else, none of them knew cats liked the place so much that they started coming back to the basement after the club was closed for the night. The cats went there to interact with one another and have a good time. Then, when the club was closed by the police because the people were making too much noise upstairs, the cats took over the basement, and it became their favorite hangout.

Khari opened her office there because Dierk's Street was a prime location for everyone to meet. From the news Khari's assistants were able to gather from their many sources, even some mice, they learned that the priests were planning to transfer Hebony from his jail cell at sunrise the next day and take him to the mummy factory where he would be killed and then, later in the day, his dead body would be brought into the city and put on display in the park down under the hill that Hebony had climbed up to see where the people were taking their cat mummies.

The path up the hill washed out in a rare rainstorm, so the festival park was closed. The priests had to use the smaller park down near the chariot hitching post. It was there that the priests would celebrate his capture and demise. That was good to know, but the cats needed to know more before they could be sure they could pull off his escape without any mistakes. If they didn't, they would have already taken his dead body to that park, and then all would have been lost. It would be too late. Hebony would have already been executed by then.

So Khari sent her reporters out again to learn what they could about any other plans the priests may have made. Some of the reporters were friends of the cats the priests kept in their homes and when they told these cats what the priests were up to, they were more than happy to listen in on whatever the priests were discussing, and then share what they'd heard. When the reporters learned what the priest's cats told them, they came back to Khari's office and put all the data they'd found together. Now they had all the information they needed to make a plan that would free Hebony from the hands of the priests. Before the priests had a chance to kill him.

It seemed the priests were planning to send an armored chariot pulled by two horses to the door of the jail at sunrise the next day. They were going to send two guards to escort Hebony to the seat of the chariot, chain him to the seat, get back into the chariot themselves, and have the driver take them to the mummy factory where he would be executed for his crimes.

More information came in a little later, and it gave Khari and her friends at the CGS the final step in their plan. The chariot was going to be pulled by two horses. They already knew the location of his pickup and the time it would happen. Horses pulling the chariot put the icing on the cake, and the cats were overjoyed. They knew that the mice would spook the horses. So, they found the mice who had been watching Hebony at his first trial and asked them to repay their favor.

The mice were more than willing to repay the favor, and they went on to say that they would find more mice to join them. They wanted to be able to super bedazzle the horses, scare the daylights out of them, make them both rear up and break loose from the chariot, and run far, far away.

When the plan was relayed to the cats that had been speaking with Hebony at the tower, he was told that everything would go well as long as he was compliant, didn't resist the guards or try to escape on his own. Hebony didn't get much sleep that night. Now his only thoughts were about freedom.

*****

Just before sunrise, the next morning, the chariot arrived at the jail to pick up Hebony and whisk him away to the mummy factory, execute him, and bring the body to a festival in Alexandria. Khari and the cats were watching the road while the mice hid in the bushes near the hitching post. When the two-horse chariot pulled up the door of the jail, the two prison guards brought Hebony from the jail and put him on the seat behind the driver. But before the guards had time to chain him to the seat, the cats gave the command to the mice, and a whole nest of them ran under the horses' feet.

The horses reared up into the air, whinnied, broke loose from the chariot, and ran off down the street. Amid the chaos, Hebony jumped off the chariot and onto the pavement, joined the other cats, and they all ran far out into the countryside as the guards and the driver stood by an empty chariot without any horses to pull it. Now Hebony was free, but this isn't the of his story. So be sure you read the next few chapters.

# CHAPTER 54

# The Events That Followed His Escape

It isn't over until the fat cat sings.

Had the plan the priests made worked out for them, the guards would have been able to take Hebony to the mummy factory and execute him for his crimes. Then they would have brought his dead body to the City of Alexandria where his corpse would have been put on display as the centerpiece for the two-day long ceremony honoring the priests for convicting him for his crimes and putting him to death.

But the first step in their plan had failed. Hebony had escaped.

But lucky for the guards, all of this had taken place when there weren't any people around. So the guards were able to capture the horses, calm them down, hitch them to the chariot again, and drive back to the mummy factory without their prisoner and without anybody knowing about their mistake. This gave them the chance to find another cat and cover up their mistake from the priests. The priests didn't know that Hebony had escaped, so they went ahead with their plans. Had they known, they would have called off the festival and sent their armies in search for Hebony and the ones who made it happen. Then that would have made this story have a very sad and different ending.

So when the guards arrived back at the mummy factory, they found another cat to bring into town in place of Hebony. This would keep them out of trouble so long as no one knew the difference. The cat they'd found was an old pet that belonged to one of the guards. He loved his cat very much, but he knew it was dying, so he put it out of its misery, and the three of them carefully turned the guard's old cat into a body double that would be a stand-in for Hebony. But this presented another problem to them. The guard's cat was a sand-color tabby, and almost everybody knew now that Hebony was black. So they came up with a clever solution. They covered the sandy color cat's fur with charcoal to make it look black, and when the cat was put on display at the festival, nobody knew the difference.

Hebony's body double fooled the priests and all the other people who saw it. Some of the festival's merrymakers took the time to walk past the body, lower their heads, and pray for him and for their own forgiveness. Others spat on it, and some petted his fur. The ones who petted its fur came away with charcoal on their hands, but none of them asked where it came from.

When the first day of the festival was over, the priests sent the body double back to the factory to be mummified and then returned the next morning when it would be put up at an auction to pay for the work of the guards, the mummification process, and to pay the court costs of his trial. By then, the residue of the charcoal or the color of the cat didn't matter because the mummy was wrapped in brown cotton mummy cloth.

# CHAPTER 55

# So How Did the Cat Mummy Find Its Way to a Cat Museum in America?

Mysteries breed mysteries.

Well, early in the morning of the second day of the festival, the mummified body of the guard's cat arrived at the festival grounds where the priests had made the arrangements for the auction. As the crowd was assembling, potential bidders examined the mummy, asked questions about it, talked with their friends about how much they were willing to bid, and waited for the auction to begin. When the gavel went down, some of the bystanders, a number of priests, a young man from a faraway country, and a beautiful woman who looked a lot like the lady at Hebony's trial were all ready to start the bidding.

Some of them said that they would bid whatever it took to win a mummy that they thought was Hebony's body. The bidding was fast and heated, and it brought much interest from the crowd. The woman, who now looked more like the one that had defended Hebony, and the young man from far away were both bidding on the mummy with back-to-back bids. He would bid, and then she would bid higher. Soon, the two of them had raised the price up higher than the budget of the priest or anyone else who might have wanted to bid. And when it was all over, the young man had won and owned the mummy, and the woman went away very mad.

But later in the day, she thought better and went to speak with the young man. They had lunch together. She asked him to date her, and after a whirlwind romance, she asked him to marry her, and she became his third wife. When her newly acquired husband suddenly died a few months later from very suspicious causes, she inherited the mummy and all of his money. Using some of his money, for tuition, she went to college and became a druggist, and as a sideline, she became a dealer in fine antique Egyptian lace. But when the market for Egyptian lace crashed, she had to sell the mummy to pay her rent, and soon after that, she died from drinking some unknown substance.

Not that it mattered then, but after her death, her maid found several bottles of arsenic in her dresser-drawer, and she turned them over to the police because she thought that the content in these bottles might have been the reason for her death and of the untimely deaths of all of her other husbands. But the police had no interest in the bottles or their contents because before her death, she had been dating the chief of police. He had seen the bottles, he knew that arsenic smelled like almond nuts, and he wasn't about to drink any of her tea.

Later, the owner of a little shop in Alexandria went to the young woman's estate sale and bought the mummy along with a few other items she liked. From there, the mummy, who everyone still thought was Hebony, made its way to Rome and then on to what was then known as Gaul. Many years later, it ended up in London. There it was sold to a tourist from America who brought it home to Brooklyn, New York, and I bought it from his estate after he had died.

Now the mummy is on display in The American Museum of the House Cat near Sylva, North Carolina.

# CHAPTER 56

# The Lives of Hebony and Khari
# after He Made His Escape

As most old stories go, they were to live happily ever after.

After the escape, Khari went back to live under the house where she lived before she met Hebony. She lived there until someone told her they knew where Hebony was hiding, and she joined him deep in the forest. They lived there together and made many, many kittens. And Hebony, to his word, helped her raise each and every one of them. He was a good father and thought it was something that all male cats should do, but alas, it never caught on. So he spent his time teaching their kittens to be aware of the value of the land and to never leave their waste on top of the ground like the people do. "Cats," he would say, "always bury their waste in a hole they dug before they made it." This way their poop is out of sight, nobody will step in it and it will be able to decay and enrich the soil. Hebony may have been without a doubt the land's first ecology teacher.

When the both of them became too old to have more kittens, she and Hebony helped younger cats raise their kittens, and Hebony began calling himself a "He-Mamma-Cat." He never returned to his home in the Hitter lands, and he never saw his mother again. But one day, much later in his life, Hebony's brother, Aten, appeared out of the blue.

They greeted, shook paws, and then Hebony said, "Aten, I have a joke for you. How do you get a mouse to come up out of his hole?"

Aten smiled and replied, "You put peas around the hole, and when the mouse comes up to take a pea, you pounce on him. That's an old, old joke, my brother."

Hebony smiled and nodded his head.

Then they both laughed over it and spent the rest of the day talking to one another. But they never brought up anything about their past. It was just like nothing had ever happened between them. They were like two brothers again. But it was rumored at the time that Aten remained in Egypt and became involved in the Battle of Actium, a war between Egypt and Rome, and he could turn up another book.

Hebony lived to be over two hundred cat years, and he lived longer than the Egyptian empire. He died of a coronavirus infection, and no one knows where his unmarked grave is located. May he rest in peace.

# CHAPTER 57

# Why Did the Priests Make Cat Mummies?

Read on; the answer is clear.

I think it was because their empire was under attack from many sides, and the people didn't know what to do. It seemed to them that their gods had forsaken them. Their god was a female cat. So the priests thought they could impress her and make life better for themselves by giving her the offering of a mummified cat.

# Author's Notes

I hope I was able to suspend the truth enough to depict little house cats as people, and at the same time, have not done a disservice to the cat.

As Mark Twain once said, "Of all God's creatures, there is only one that cannot be made the slave of the lash. That one is the cat. If man could be crossed with the cat, it would improve man, but it would deteriorate the cat."

I am both a retired professor of biology and a scientist, but I would never want to have it said that I have done anything that would degrade the cat. I admire the cat.

Before becoming a teacher, I was a marine biologist for the State of Florida, working on marine research and mariculture, the study of farming the sea. After that, I wrote environmental impact statements on construction projects along the shoreline, in valuable wetlands, and on beaches and offshore barrier islands. All of these had values of their own. These were the places where immature sea life grew up, and the beaches and barrier islands protected the mainland.

The goal of these studies was to stem or, better yet, stop these building projects and save the sea. Most studies were thrown out by the courts because a judge ruled in favor of economic benefits and said that the projects were worth more to the builders than to the people who made their living catching fish from the sea or the people who had used the shoreline for recreation. All in all, my studies were a waste of my time and for the money spent by the Florida Department of Natural Resources that paid me.

Teaching gave me the chance to educate young people about the values of nature and the benefits these areas along the shoreline would have provided had they been left as they were.

I lectured to more than two thousand students a year for twenty-two years. It wasn't until I retired in 1991 that I found my love for cats.

After retirement, my wife and I moved to rural western North Carolina, and we discovered that the animal shelters there didn't have much interest in saving cats.

They told me it was dog country. So I made it my mission to change that. I got to know cats a lot better, and I became interested in helping them and became more appreciated.

Because I was unable to find any local shelters that would change their mind and do so, in 1996, I opened a small private cat shelter in a converted tool shed. Later, when I inherited some money, I built the Catman2 Shelter near Cullowhee, North Carolina.

Since it opened in 2002, it has rescued thousands of stray cats and all the cats people brought me.

Today, the shelter also rehabilitates injured wildlife.

Soon after I opened the cat shelter, something told me that there was a need for a museum for the house cats, and I started dreaming of the day I would open one. For years, my wife and I traveled the eastern United States, finding all the objects I wanted in a first-class museum. When eBay and auctions came along, we bought more items there.

We waited, we stored things away, and we collected.

Then in 2016, I was offered space for a museum in a local antique mall, and in 2017, The American Museum of the House Cat opened, and it operated there until the mall closed in 2019.

But I'd saved some money left over from a house I'd sold when I moved to another, and the profit provided me enough cash needed to build my own building for the museum.

My cash windfalls seemed to come just at the right time. And they came by just plain, dumb luck. You don't get rich on a teacher's salary. I lived at a good time to make money.

But I am happy I was able to spend that money on the cat shelter and the museum. The cat museum was the rainbow at the end of a long dream, and I would do it again if I had to.

Somebody once said, "No one should be judged by how much money they die with, but by how much money they give away for the benefit of others before they died."

My windfalls came before I died. They built a cat shelter and a cat museum. And I would do it all over again. You can learn more about my cat shelter and cat museum if you google them on your laptop or computer. For more information about both of them, see a webpage and a Facebook listing for both: wnccatmuseum.com and Catman2.org. I hope you will help support the cat museum by donating a little money every now and then. Please remember the cat museum in your will. I built the cat museum for the people that love cats and I have, in no way, profited from it. Museums don't have a lot of income, but every year this museum tries to transfer a little money from its profits to the Catman2 Shelter to help fund its low-to-no-cost spay and neuter program and feral cat control. The museum would also appreciate help from the corporations and businesses that profit from the sales of cat-related products, such as cat food, litter, and all the other items cat lovers buy for their cats. The museum is planning to introduce a trust fund that will help to secure the museum's future. It is one of only two cat museums in America and one of only nine in the whole world. It would be a shame if it were to close because of a lack of funding, and I doubt if there would ever be another. Myself, all the cat people, and all the cats I know, thank you in advance. Dr. Harold W. Sims Jr., I will help support both as long as I live. After that, it's up to you. Do it for the cats.

Travel around the world, fancy cars, houses, and the like are made of dust, and their memories die with you, and few will care to hear of them. So have a dream and leave something that will live on after you when you die. That's the best way to go.

The End

# About the Author

Dr. Harold Walter Sims Jr. was born in Mount Vernon, New York, in 1935. Being born during the depression, his early life was of a little interest.

In 1940, his family moved to a small farming community in Sempronius, New York, and attended a one-room school then went to Moravia Central High School and graduated in 1953. He was a poor student and graduated near the bottom in class. After a semester at Cortland State Teachers' College, he ran out of money after one semester and joined the US Navy to get the GI Bill. He served three years, was discharged, and three years graduated from Florida State University in 1962, just shy of a master's degree. He was married in 1962 to Kay

Sims, who was his wife for fifty-nine years. Kay died in 2021. His first job was with the Florida Department of Natural Resources. His first assignment was to convert an old rail road camp's mess hall into a salt-water laboratory and made an attempt to raise spiny lobsters a farm-like way. He'd had experience raising both crabs and shellfish at FSU, but it seemed that the spiny lobster was a slow-growing animal and needed more than nine months to reach an eatable size. A year later, he was transferred to the marine laboratory and spent the next four years working with shellfish and writing scientific papers on spiny lobsters, clams, and oysters.

One of the twenty-three papers, a paper about the spiny lobster, earned him a Best Paper of the Year award from the Florida Academy of Sciences. He left the marine lab four years later and returned to FSU. He earned a master's degree in junior college teaching after a job as a sanitarian and worked for the Department of Natural Resources writing environmental impact statements for building permits along the Florida shoreline. Most of the permits were granted because a local judge saw the development more important than marine life.

In 1962, he landed a job at St. Petersburg Junior College in Clearwater and transferred a biology class into a class of ecology and has to write a book to teach it because, prior to that, ecology was taught as a mathematical science of models rather than a subject about the natural environment, including people. While teaching there, he earned his doctor's degree and left there in 1991.

Soon after that, he volunteered at a local animal shelter and began his lifelong interest in house cats. When he moved to North Carolina to find the county where he found the local cats in need of care, he opened a small cat shelter. In 1962, he built and opened the four-thousand-square-foot Catman2 cats, cats only shelter a facility without cages. It is still open and has added a small animal rescue center that takes care of injured and abandoned wildlife. Then seeing a need for a cat museum in America, with his own money as he had with the cat shelter, in 2017 he opened the American Museum of the House Cat in Sylva, North Carolina. It is one of two cat museums in America and of nine in the world.

Harold's money came from working hard for forty years before retirement, saving it when interest rates at banks was over 10 percent, savings paid off, a rather large inheritance from a great aunt, a large sale of a home near Cashiers, and frugal-living—no expensive foreign travel and when traveling in America, never staying in a lodge any better than Day's Inn. He has never asked for rent from the cat shelter nor cat museum because he feels giving is better than taking.

He has published four books about cats and has written articles about them in major cat magazines. *Hebony's Odyssey*, taking him more than four years to finish, is his first novel. By the time this book is published, Harold will be eighty-eight years old but hopes to write another book Hebony and his brother, Aten, where they become involved with the Battle of Actium in which the Egyptian empire is invaded by the Romans and an empire of more than nine thousand years is defeated. The war has many colorful characters such as Queen Cleopatra, Mark Anthony, and host in thousands of troops from both sides.

Harold will be 87 years old.